WILD IS THE DAY

Wild is the Day

Christine Marion Fraser

This edition published 1998 by Pan Books
an imprint of Macmillan Publishers Ltd,
25 Eccleston Place, London SW1W 9NF
and Basingstoke

Associated companies throughout the world

1 2 3 4 5 6 7 8 9

This first world edition published in Great Britain 1996 by
SEVERN HOUSE PUBLISHERS LTD of
9-15 High Street, Sutton, Surrey SM1 1DF.
First published in the USA 1997 by
SEVERN HOUSE PUBLISHERS INC., of
595 Madison Avenue, New York, NY 10022.

British Library Cataloguing in Publication Data

Fraser, Christine Marion
  Wild is the day
  1. English fiction – 20th century – Scottish authors
  2. Scottish fiction – 20th century
  I. Title
  823.9'14 [F]

  ISBN 0 330 37420 6

Typeset by Palimpsest Book Production Limited,
Polmont, Stirlingshire
Printed and bound in Great Britain by
Mackays of Chatham plc, Chatham, Kent

For Jennifer
who discovered the 'Wardrobe' novels.

Chapter One

Lucy watched the bus receding over the narrow winding road till it became just a dot in the misted purple of the December dusk, and a strange feeling of desolation washed over her. This was it, she was at her destination, Ardben village on the Kintyre coast – at least – she was almost there – she still had to find her way to Moorgate House. Dr Lorn Campbell had said in his letter he would meet her at the post office around four. A glance at her watch told her it was ten minutes past that hour and there was no sign of anyone outside the green corrugated tin hut that was Ardben Post Office.

Behind it, the hills soared, aloof and mysterious in the gathering darkness; a cold little breeze blew skittishly through the glen, making her shiver slightly. She had been on the bus from Glasgow since ten that morning and during the journey had felt heavy with weariness, though her first sight of the snowcapped Scottish hills had lifted her spirits and for the first time since leaving Leeds she had felt a surge of anticipation pulsing in her veins.

Now, gazing over the blue-grey sea, she felt a bleakness in her heart such as she had never known before. It was stronger even than the dreadful loneliness that had gnawed inside her since her break-up with Allan six weeks ago.

Six weeks! It seemed an eternity. At the time she'd thought that life itself had stood still.

His face floated into her mind, his boyish good looks, his small boy innocent charm. Innocent! That was hardly an apt description of him. Not now that she knew the real Allan Graham, had found him in the arms of another woman after he had promised his undying love to her. She had known that she had to get away – away from hopes, dreams, broken promises . . .

A memory of that earth-shattering scene floated unbidden into her mind. The bed in his flat where he and she had made such wonderful love and so many exciting plans for the future, occupied by another woman whom she'd never set eyes on before. Everything had been mussed and ruffled, the sheets, the pillows, the duvet. She remembered the whiteness of the woman's naked limbs; the expression on her face when her dazed eyes had focused on the doorway to see Lucy standing there in stunned shock, watching everything in mesmerised horror before taking to her heels as fast as her shaking legs would allow.

And later, when he had come looking for her to try and patch things up between them, telling her that the other woman had meant nothing to him, it was just something that had happened, she had thrown herself at him and wouldn't take no for an answer. He had said that nothing like it would happen again, that surely, if she truly loved him as she had said, she should find it in her heart to forgive him.

He had been persuasive, tender, remorseful, and it had taken every shred of her willpower to resist him, especially when he had taken her into his arms and had tried to kiss away her protests with that warm, firm, exciting mouth of his.

2

At that point she had almost succumbed to him but she had struggled and had pushed him away and he had stood back to look at her with the melting reproach of a large rejected puppy dog who didn't quite understand what it had done that was so terrible.

"I'm a very loving man, Lucy," he had said as if that excused everything. "I didn't deliberately encourage that girl but she was lonely and I felt sorry for her. She only wanted a bit of comfort." He had spread his hands in appeal then, a rueful little smile hovering at the corners of his mouth, and it had struck her then how little she really knew about him, except that he originally came from a remote part of Scotland, though he said he didn't get home very often. He had been enthusiastic talking to her about his Scottish roots and she had been enchanted by his descriptions of his homeland.

But there hadn't been much else. Right from the start he had been something of an enigma: he'd never introduced her to any of his friends, had seldom taken her anywhere worth mentioning, making the excuse that he wanted to have her all to himself, that he was jealous of the very thought of another man daring to look at her.

She had been so besotted by him she had gladly fallen in with anything he wanted to do. She didn't want to share him either; it was wonderful the way it was, just the two of them, dining together in his flat, feeling that they were the only two people in the whole wide world, a world of delight, of love, of precious hours spent in each other's company.

That was why she had taken his treachery so badly, why she knew she had to get away from him and start a whole new way of life for herself. After all, she told herself resolutely, life didn't begin and end with Allan

Graham. Before she had met him she'd had a full and busy social life with plenty of boyfriends, though none of them serious.

From as far back as she could recall she had wanted to be a nurse and she had never wavered from that ambition. She had done her stint as a probationer in a big, busy hospital and had worked her way up to a senior position with a lot of responsibilities. For a time she had been a health visitor but in recent years she had gone in for private nursing. That was what had given her the idea of trying to find a position as far away from Allan as possible.

"Don't let the likes of him drive you away, lass," her mother had told her firmly but soon afterwards she paid a visit to a nursing agency and the girl there had said she might have the very thing to suit her requirements.

"It's in Scotland," she had said, smiling at Lucy as she went on, "a place called Ardben, on the Kintyre coast."

Lucy had drawn in her breath at that point. Scotland! The country of Allan's birth. Surely she couldn't even begin to dream of working there! But then she had given herself a little mental shake. What was she thinking of? Scotland wasn't simply a tiny dot on a map. It was bigger than anyone who had not been there would have imagined. She had holidayed there a few times and had fallen in love with the wildness and the grandeur of the place. The chances of meeting Allan there were very slim indeed – yet – the Kintyre coast – hadn't he mentioned an area like that when he was telling her about his birthplace? And Ardben village? It sounded familiar . . . If she accepted this post would she be subconsciously seeking out his birthplace? Punishing herself by going to work in the very places in which he had wandered as a young boy?

4

But no! She shrugged the notion away. It was just a coincidence, that was all, surely? She struggled to remember what he'd said about his family. It hadn't been much, in fact, now that she thought about it, he had been evasive and really quite secretive on that score. . . . He had been enthusiastic about the Scottish countryside but his family hadn't appeared very much in the landscape. . . .

"Can you tell me a little bit more about it?" she had heard herself saying with fast-beating heart, and the girl had readily supplied her with more information.

"The client's name is Lorn Campbell, he's a country GP and is looking for a nurse-companion for his invalid wife; preferably someone young and cheerful with a steady disposition and enough common sense to be able to deal with any awkward situations that might arise."

"Awkward situations?" Lucy intervened at that juncture. "Sounds as if Mrs Campbell might be a bit of a handful."

"Mmm, it doesn't say that of course," the girl hedged. "It would only be for a trial period anyway. You don't have to commit yourself right away."

"All right." Lucy made the decision quickly before she could change her mind. "I'll do it. No time like the present for taking the bull by the horns. I need a complete change in my life and this could very well be it."

The answer to her application had come surprisingly quickly, accepting her for a trial period on the strength of the references she had given the agency. Now here she was, far from home and feeling very alone, but she wasn't going to give herself time to think along these lines.

Resolutely she straightened her slim shoulders. She would show everyone what she was made of. These last few weeks she had worn a mask of composure so that even

5

those nearest her had been fooled into thinking her heart was healing – all except her parents. They had watched her with a sadness in their eyes, and when she announced her intention of going off to a new post in Scotland they had accepted the news quietly. Her father's last words, as he hugged her close, seemed to breathe softly in the sigh of the wind. "You take care, lass, and remember, if things don't go right you know your bed will always be waiting."

A tear choked in her throat but with a little shake of impatience she lifted her heavy suitcases and walked towards the glimmer of light that shone from the post office window. Inside was a stout, cheery-looking woman who, at Lucy's entrance, scuttled hurriedly to the counter as if to prove she had been busily employed there since the bus had dropped off the mail, instead of which she had been peering wonderingly from the window at Lucy standing so lost-looking at the roadside.

"The mist is coming down," the woman observed in a soft, pleasant, voice, looking over her spectacles at Lucy standing in the post office premises with a rather forlorn air about her.

"Yes. I was wondering, can you tell me how to get to Moorgate House? Dr Campbell said he would meet me here but there's no sign of him."

"Ach well," the woman folded her arms and, leaning forward, she rested them on a pile of newspapers sitting on the counter, "he will likely have been called out – poor man. There is a lot of 'flu about and no doubt he'll be kept busy running about seeing to everyone. I hear from your accent that you're from Yorkshire. We get a lot of young men from there in the summer, for the fishing. Are you visiting up yonder at Moorgate House?"

A guarded curiosity had swamped her homely features and Lucy smiled. How well she knew the look. Having been born and brought up in a small rural community, where the sight of a stranger made everyone agog, she was used to such curiosity and this woman was unwittingly making her feel at home.

She wore nothing to indicate that she was a nurse. *I would be grateful if you didn't wear uniform* . . . Dr Campbell had written . . . *my wife will feel more at ease if you dress as for everyday.*

It was obvious from the postmistress's question that the doctor was a private sort of person, but Lucy saw no reason to hide anything. It would be all over the village in a matter of hours anyway. The postmistress received the news with a knowing kind of nod.

"I am not surprised at all; he would get the moon for that wife of his if he could. You're not the first, mind, there have been others but none of them have stuck it for more than a week or two. A tragedy that – her landing up the way she is. My, she was a bonny woman before – well, you'll hear all about that soon enough. No one can accuse me of being a gossip but och, none of us will ever forget how she was. Blithe as a skylark, always flitting around." She looked conspiratorially over her spectacles at Lucy, "Flighty, some would say . . ."

Lucy moved her cold feet impatiently. "Could you tell me how to get to Moorgate House – Mrs . . . ?"

"MacSporran – but just call me Jessie, everyone does."

Lucy almost burst out laughing. MacSporran! It was wonderfully, beautifully Scottish.

Jessie MacSporran looked at her searchingly. "You have a sprite in your eye, my lassie, but you look tired all the same. I tell you what, you just take with you what you'll need for the present and I'll get my man to bring over the heavy suitcases either tonight or first thing tomorrow. Come with me to the door and I'll show you where to go."

Chapter Two

A few minutes later Lucy was trudging up the road. The mist had blotted out the sea and the hills, closing her into a small world of grey road, springy turf and the looming ghostly shapes of wind-twisted trees. Soft lights glowed from the curtained-off windows of roadside cottages, but these soon petered out, and now it was just the odd glint from a distant croft or farmhouse.

Half a mile out of the village the road wound through the moors and a little tremor of apprehension fluttered in her stomach. It was almost pitch black now and she didn't even have a torch. She was cold and weary and with every step she took the coil of nerves inside her grew tighter and tighter.

"Little more than half a mile," had beamed Jessie MacSporran but Lucy felt she had been trudging the countryside for hours.

The purr of a car at her back made her jump and step quickly onto the verge. The car slowed and stopped beside her and a pale blur of a face appeared at the window. "I met Jessie MacSporran at the post office and she told me you had started to walk. I'm Dr Campbell. I'm sorry I missed you, I was called out. If you had waited just a few more minutes . . ." There was a slight reproach in a voice otherwise utterly beautiful in all its lilting charm.

God bless Jessie MacSporran, thought Lucy as she climbed into the passenger seat and put her overnight case in the back. The car moved forward and she searched her mind for something to say but there was nothing. Dr Campbell too was silent and it was this very quietness of his that seemed to reach out and enshroud them both. He was a dark figure at her side, concentrating everything into driving the car through the mist which curled eerily over the moors and blanketed them in a little world of their own, and so aware was she of his presence that the coil in her belly became so tight she felt sick.

"You must be tired."

His words made her jump and she nodded, then, feeling foolish because she realised he couldn't possibly see the gesture, she answered tightly, "Yes, I am, it's been a long day."

"Well, we're here now." He swung the car through a pair of heavy wooden gates and up the driveway. The house was huddled darkly against the darker hills but lights shone warmly in the downstairs rooms and Lucy, unaware till that moment that she had been holding her breath, let it go with a soft little sigh.

He got out and went round to open the door for her then he opened the front door of the house and called, "Nora, Miss Pemberton is here. Will you show her in while I put the car away?"

A slender immaculate woman with lavender-tinted hair, appeared in the doorway. Lucy held out her hand but there was no response and immediately she sensed resentment. Like a living thing it rushed out to meet her and slowly she withdrew her hand and let it fall to her side.

"Miss Pemberton," acknowledged the woman in high, very polite tones. "How do you do. I am Mrs Bruce, Dr

10

Campbell's mother-in-law. Do come in, you must be cold and weary."

The interior of the house was unlike anything Lucy could ever have imagined as the residence of a country doctor. She stepped from the hall into the lounge and felt as if she had just walked into the pages of a glossy magazine. The room was spacious and bright, filled with elegant white furniture and expensive fittings. Immediately she felt uncomfortable and out of place and she wanted to turn and run back to her parents' farm in Yorkshire. If she had combed her hair, if only she had done that before getting out of the car . . . but she hadn't, and she was acutely aware of it clinging damply round her head.

Involuntarily she turned and almost collided with the doctor. He put a hand under her arm to steady her. For a moment his face was very near her own and for no reason that she could fathom her heart began to race madly.

For the first time she saw what he looked like: tall, too thin, brown hair, a lock of it curling over his brow. His was a sensitive fine-boned face with a firm, well-shaped mouth . . . and his eyes – she could hardly tear her own away from them, for they were like umber forest pools, remote, cool, yet in that brief moment of touching her she fancied a lifting of the veil, for there was a gentleness in them as he looked at her tired young face and saw the expression of uncertainty gazing starkly out of her own blue-grey eyes.

"Go on in, Miss Pemberton," he told her courteously. "I will show you to your room once you have rested. No doubt you would like to freshen up after your long journey."

There was something about the way he spoke, in a

11

guarded manner, as if he had grown used to hiding his true self from the world. The soft lights found the hollows in his face; a weariness lay deep in his eyes; there was dejection in the droop of his shoulders which were broad, despite his lean appearance.

Nora Bruce was standing at the fireplace, her hands folded primly over her stomach, watching as Lucy was ushered in, making no attempt to come forward or help in any way. She glanced at Lucy sideways. "I'll go and see about some tea. No doubt you need it, Miss Pemberton. We don't have dinner until eight which will give you a chance to settle into your room."

Lucy was left with the doctor in the middle of the lounge. The house was very warm and the heat, coming after the fresh cold of the December evening, brought a flush to her smooth cheeks. She felt breathless and strange and put out a hand to the back of a chair to steady herself. A wave of faintness washed over her and she lowered her head. Fool! Fool, that she was! She should have had something to eat earlier but hadn't felt hungry. She hadn't felt like eating for weeks now, not since Allan . . .

"Are you alright, Miss Pemberton?" Dr Campbell's voice broke sharply into her fuzzing brain.

"Yes – I – it's just the heat after the cold – also, I haven't eaten."

"Sit down," he ordered firmly. "I'll get Nora to bring that tea now. A warm drink is obviously what you need – after all, we must have you quite fit to look after my wife; you'll need all your strength for that." Turning on his heel he went abruptly out of the room.

Was she mistaken or had his voice held a vibrant note of sarcasm? She didn't know, she was so weary, and she

12

asked herself if she had made the right decision coming here. He was right. She was a nurse; nurses were supposed always to be strong, ready for anything. She felt none of these things and she was afraid now that she wasn't yet ready to face up to reality.

Her shoulders drooped and she put a slender hand to her eyes. The door opened again and Nora Bruce came in with a tea trolley which she placed in front of Lucy. There was no sign of the doctor. Lucy wished he would come back. Somehow she didn't want to be alone in the same room as his mother-in-law.

"My son-in-law has gone to take evening surgery," said the older woman flatly, as if she had read the girl's mind. She poured two cups of tea, handing one to Lucy, laying her own on a smoked glass table as she busied herself with plates. "Help yourself to a sandwich, Miss Pemberton," she went on politely, then, satisfied that she had carried out her duties, she sat herself down on a settee opposite to the one occupied by Lucy.

Lucy picked up a dainty morsel from her plate but found the food sticking in her throat. She was acutely aware that the older woman was watching her with a keen scrutiny, but several minutes elapsed before Nora Bruce's clear, high voice broke the silence. "I do not approve of your coming here, you know, Miss Pemberton. There have been others before you but they soon left. I thought Lorn had got over his silly notions about having outsiders in the house – a companion for Clarrissa indeed!"

Lucy was so taken aback she said nothing, but a flush of humiliation was spreading rapidly over her fair skin.

"I am perfectly capable of looking after my daughter in my own way." The voice of Nora Bruce was softer now. "I don't know what on earth Lorn is thinking about – bringing strange young women into this house. He didn't tell me that he had applied to that nursing agency, just sneaked around arranging things behind our backs. 'Clarrissa must have someone young to keep her company', that's what he told me afterwards and to think I gave up my home – everything – to come here and look after her when she almost died giving birth to his child. I warned him, I told him she wasn't strong enough to have children, but of course – men! Selfish! Only think of themselves."

Lucy raised her head and looked the older woman straight in the face, noting the critical, restless dark eyes, the discontented mouth, and she knew that here, before she had even started, was an enemy. She stood up. "If you don't mind, I'd like to go to my room, Mrs Bruce. I must tidy myself up."

Nora Bruce glanced at the girl's fair halo of hair clinging in damp tiny tendrils round her head and she stretched her lips into a sneering smile. "Yes, of course, dear, you do look rather rumpled. Clarrissa wouldn't like to see you in such a state."

She patted her lavender head affectedly. "She's beautiful you know – oh, she could have had anybody! Such looks, gaiety, talent, style. Men fell at her feet, Miss Pemberton, men who would have cherished her and given her the sort of life a girl like her needs. But she was always too stubborn for her own good and wouldn't listen to me when I tried to give her advice. She always got her own way no matter what I said. She desperately wanted Dr Campbell, and of course, she got him. Clarrissa always saw the romance in everything; she pictured herself as a country doctor's wife but the novelty soon wore off.

14

But by then it was too late, she fell pregnant . . . and now! Oh, my poor darling . . .!"

Lucy couldn't stand another minute of Nora Bruce. She wanted only to escape, and hastily she turned away, stumbling on the head of a tiger-skin rug in her hurry to leave the room.

". . . She had such bearing, such grace . . ." The high voice was going on and on. Lucy wrenched at the door handle just as it was turned from the other side and the doctor looked in.

"I left my phone messages here . . ." His keen gaze took in the scene at a glance: Lucy's crimson face, Nora Bruce's equally heated countenance, but he just said quietly, "I have a few moments to spare, Miss Pemberton. Mrs MacSporran gave me your cases, I have taken them up to your room. If you would care to come with me . . ."

She followed him along the wood-panelled hall and up a narrow staircase. He led her along a passageway and opened a door into a charming country bedroom with rose-sprigged walls and a polished wood floor scattered with rugs. The ceiling was oak-beamed, the furnishings shabby and comfortable looking. The huge double bed was piled high with feather mattresses and downy quilts and it was so like her own room at home she couldn't stop her exclamation of pleasure.

The doctor smiled, a smile that altered his serious face. "The whole house was originally done in the usual country fashion," he explained. "My wife changed all the rooms downstairs but never quite got round to these." He spread his hands. She noticed they were long and slender. "She can't get upstairs now of course, and has lost interest. I wanted you to sleep in the room next to

15

hers below – but her mother would not be moved – so upstairs it is I'm afraid."

"Oh, but I'm glad!" cried Lucy. "Not that I don't like it downstairs – it's just – this is so much more like home."

"Well, I hope you'll be comfortable . . ." He paused. "I'm afraid the upper floor isn't too warm. I got the central heating in for my wife, who feels the cold a lot, but we never got it extended upstairs. However, there's plenty of hot water in the bathroom and an electric fire in here if you feel chilly."

I'm glad, glad, glad! Lucy's heart sang. She hated stuffy rooms and always slept with her window open at home. She was still standing in the doorway and when he turned to go they were so near each other she could see the pulse beating in his neck, and, something she hadn't noticed before: a deep cleft in the middle of his firm chin. Her head came to just below his shoulders so that her eyes were in line with the dimple and she found herself having to repress an impulse to put the tip of her pinky into it.

He saw her staring and an odd look came into his eyes, a plea, such a glance of silent appeal that she told herself sharply to stop imagining things. This was her employer; she was here to nurse his wife – still, she couldn't get over this feeling of awareness, of being overwhelmed by him.

"The bathroom is just along the hall." His tones were clipped, coldness now hooded the emotions in his eyes. "Remember, dinner is at eight. I will talk to you later about my wife, what she will require from you – she . . . well – we'll talk later."

She heard his footsteps retreating down the passage

16

and she was alone in the room, which was at the rear of the house. The sound of the sea came to her and she went to the window to listen with pleasure to the surf breaking softly on the shore. Opening the window she breathed deeply the fresh salt-laden air and some of her inner turmoil evaporated.

Then another sound penetrated the night: voices drifting from the windows below. She recognised the doctor's soft, lilting tones, but they were being drowned in a high petulant voice which, for a moment, she thought must be that of Nora Bruce. But no, this voice was younger and she realised it must be that of the doctor's wife.

"Oh, for heaven's sake, Lorn!" The words were sharp with annoyance. "Of course I'll be on my best behaviour with my new little nanny! But I told you, I don't need anyone to hold my hand. I do wish you would stop fussing! You're worse than Mother!"

Lucy's cheeks burned. Nanny! So that was Clarrissa Campbell's attitude to her. She sank down on the edge of the bed and stared at her clasped hands. Loneliness washed over her in waves, mingling with an overwhelming feeling of homesickness. She thought of her parents. They would be having tea about now; the lovely homely farmhouse kitchen would be filled with appetising smells; she could almost hear the kettle singing on the fire, see old Bess lying in her basket, one eye on her plate to see if by chance anything had landed in it while she was asleep. . . .

Another picture floated into her mind blotting out the first – Allan, his fair head shining; his blue eyes gazing into hers, promising her his eternal love; his mouth searching and eager, drenching her senses, filling

17

her horizons with her love for him. "Oh, Allan," she whispered brokenly, and, putting her face into her hands, she wept.

Chapter Three

Lucy slowly descended the stairs. It wasn't quite eight yet but she didn't want to keep anyone waiting at table and she wasn't sure where the dining room was.

Having showered and changed into a pale green woollen dress she felt refreshed and certainly more able to face the immediate world. There was no one to be seen in the hall, but a door opened further along and Nora Bruce came towards the kitchen, her dark eyes appraising Lucy in one quick sweep. She herself was dressed in a pink chiffon evening dress and was liberally adorned with jewels. Lucy swallowed hard and thought, Oh God, they dress for dinner and I'm—

"Go along in, Miss Pemberton." The older woman's voice, clipped and cold broke into Lucy's thoughts. "I'll just go along and help Clarrissa."

The dining room was situated alongside the kitchen and was very impressive with its smoked glass oval dining table above which hung a height-adjustable glass-shaded light which spread a diffused glow over the room.

Lucy saw that the doctor was already seated, but he stood up at her entrance and went to pull out a chair. With relief she noted that he hadn't dressed up for dinner but still wore the tweed jacket and cord trousers she had seen him in earlier. He seemed to sense her thoughts for he said briefly, "I like to be comfortable, I hope you don't mind."

She laughed shakily. "Mind! I'm glad. I thought when I saw your mother-in-law that everyone except me would be all dressed up."

He smiled then, a boyish grin that transformed his whole face and made him look so much younger than she had at first imagined. He could only be in his early thirties yet at first acquaintance he had seemed older. His dark eyes flicked over her and she flushed, though she fancied approval in the look, not the silent, almost disdainful criticism she had seen in the eyes of Nora Bruce.

"You look charming the way you are," he said, and the compliment brought a smile to her own face so that it too lost its solemnity. She was a slight, rather fragile-looking girl, with shining fair curls, and big blue-grey eyes set in a heart-shaped face.

Her perfectly-shaped mouth was curved at the corners as if she had laughed a lot in her life, but since her arrival it had been rather tremulous. The smile altered it completely and for a long moment he looked at it, before pulling out her chair.

As she sat down, an odd little whining sound came from the hall accompanied by light quick footsteps. Lucy recognised the sound. She had heard it many times before: the unmistakable high drone of an electrically-propelled wheelchair. A laugh rang out, a slightly hysterical laugh followed by another, on much the same key as the first, but lower, more secretive.

Clarrissa Campbell came into the room followed by her mother, and Lucy knew that she had been the subject for their mocking merriment, for the young woman halted her chair abruptly and her eyes, dark and lustrous, immediately fell on Lucy, the amusement in them deepening as the colour in the girl's face flared yet again.

"Well, so this is my new nanny," she drawled, her long fingers curling into the golden fur of the little spaniel perched on her lap. "I've been hearing quite a lot about you."

Clarrissa Campbell was beautiful, with skin like porcelain and a mass of black hair that fell in rich waves about her face. The full mouth pouted, tiny lines of discontent marred the corners, but otherwise she was one of the most gorgeous creatures that Lucy had ever seen. She was dressed in a black evening gown that showed to startling advantage her creamy shoulders and long slender neck.

Lucy felt all at once dowdy and unattractive in such a presence and humiliated beyond measure at the mocking greeting, but her head went up and out went her firm little chin. "If you don't mind, I would rather you called me Lucy." She kept her voice steady. "And I think I should call you by your Christian name too if I'm to be your companion as well as your nurse."

Clarrissa stopped in the act of unfolding her napkin. "Lucy – how perfectly sweet – I once had a rag doll called Lucy."

There was complete silence. The doctor shifted uncomfortably and even Nora Bruce looked embarrassed by her daughter's cutting remark.

Lucy's heart was beating a tattoo in her throat but she realised it was now or never to take the bull by the horns. "Why, what a coincidence," she replied evenly. "I once had a toy rabbit called Clarrissa – rather silly of me to call it that since it had buck teeth and would have suited Tusker better . . . but then, I was only a child at the time . . ."

21

To her complete surprise the older girl threw back her head and pealed with delighted laughter. "At last, at last! Someone who can answer me back. You have quick wits for such a child."

"I'm twenty-four; not such a child. I can't be many years younger than yourself," Lucy replied.

"Five – but with me—" she indicated her chair, "like this, it could be a hundred." Clarrissa's dark eyes were shadowed as she spoke, and another silence shrouded the softly lit room, broken only by the tuneful notes of someone singing in the kitchen through the wall.

The serving hatch suddenly slammed open near Clarrissa and she said peevishly, "Really, Meg, I do wish you wouldn't do that! My nerves are frayed enough as it is."

"Sorry, lass, the damned thing is stiff and I'm in a hurry. Can I start serving now?" The cheery voice fell on Lucy's ears like notes of music and brought to the atmosphere the first hint of normality she had experienced since entering Moorgate House.

Meg Stewart was the daily help, and for the next half-hour she clattered dishes, rattled pans, served up a most delicious meal, and kept up a flow of such light-hearted chatter that any other sort was kept at bay.

Lucy watched her through the hatch and was reminded of her own mother, the round sweet face framed in a cloud of white hair; the quick smile; the natural humour.

When she set down the tray of desserts on the serving hatch bar and announced her intention of, "getting away home to see to Bob," Lucy got up impulsively and went over to get the tray.

"Thanks, Meg, that was a lovely meal," she said warmly. "It was just what I needed to buck me up after all my travelling today."

22

The woman gave her a gentle, sympathetic smile. "Ach well, I've been used to cooking and catering all my days – Miss . . . ?"

"Pemberton. But please call me Lucy."

"Ay well, Lucy, I'm glad to see you enjoying your meat." She glanced rather disapprovingly at Clarrissa who had only toyed with her meal. "I cannot abide waste, not when there's so much war and want in the world today. Now, I must away." She peeled off her apron. "Goodnight all, I'll see you in the morning."

When she had gone Nora Bruce compressed her lips. "It would be better if you didn't get too familiar with the staff, Miss Pemberton. These people love gossip and spread things about."

For almost the first time since the start of the meal the doctor spoke up. "Och, come on, Nora, Meg is hardly staff; she's been a friend of this family for years and she's an indispensable help into the bargain."

Lucy too couldn't keep quiet. "If Meg is staff – then surely I come under that category too and oughtn't to be having my meals with the family."

She might not have spoken. Nora Bruce ignored her. "Hmph," she snorted. "Indispensable? She doesn't even wait to do the dishes after serving dinner."

The doctor's jaw tensed. "That's hardly fair. She's supposed to stop at four, yet she comes back here after tea to help with all the rigmarole of our evening meal. Also she's got Bob to see to . . ."

"My pills," Clarrissa said, rummaging through her bag. "I do wish you two would stop bickering and help me find my pills. I was sure I had some in here."

The doctor was up like a shot. "I'll get you some, darling, I put them in the bathroom cabinet."

"Which is out of my reach! Lorn, why do you treat me like a baby? Why do you, Lorn? Are you afraid I might do something nasty – take an overdose? Something like that?"

Her voice had risen alarmingly and he went to stand behind her, his fingers gently massaging the smooth skin of her shoulders. "Darling, please don't, I'll get the pills for you at once. Your shoulders are cold, I'll fetch a wrap from your room." His hand brushed against the dark hair at her neck but impatiently she pushed him away.

He loves her, Lucy thought. Oh God, how he loves her, and she seems to resent him for it.

Nora Bruce began clearing the dishes away and Lucy offered to help. "No!" The refusal was sharp. "I can manage. You had better get on with what you came here to do. You and Clarrissa ought to get to know one another. I'll bring coffee through to the sitting room."

The phone shrilled as Lucy followed Clarrissa out to the hall. Shortly afterwards the doctor came to the sitting room to take his wife's hands in his. "I've got to go out, darling, I hope you don't mind. I wanted to spend this first evening with you and Miss Pemberton."

Lucy thought how tired he looked, with an exhaustion deep in his brown eyes, but Clarrissa gave him no sympathy. "Mind! Why should I mind? I've spent almost every night alone since our marriage, Lorn dear."

"There's a lot of 'flu in the neighbourhood at the moment, Clarrissa. I must go where I'm needed."

She laughed bitterly. "Of course – 'flu, measles, chills, they're all out there waiting for you, Lorn. Everyone needs you! It doesn't matter that I might need you more than anyone."

Lucy turned away for she couldn't bear to see the hurt

darkening those brown eyes of his. With her he had been cold; a look that was almost resentment had been an ugly expression in eyes that were so full of compassion and tenderness when he looked at his wife.

He was like putty in her hands. Lucy had noticed it from the first moment Clarrissa appeared. She sneered at him, derided him, regardless of who was present and not once did he raise his voice in anger to her.

Lucy watched him tuck a mohair stole round her shoulders and bend to kiss her but she turned her face away and left him. He paused in front of Lucy, his bag clutched in his hand, and now he was Dr Campbell once more, the strange, silent man who had sat beside her in the car, aloof and unapproachable.

"If you are still up when I get back, I will talk to you, Miss Pemberton." His voice was very distant and he didn't look at her. "I am not taking the car, the croft I have to visit is not far from here so I shouldn't be very long. Let Nora see my wife into bed tonight – you can start your duties after you have had a night's rest."

Lucy heard him with one ear; with the other she heard the rain hissing down outside. Automatically she picked up an umbrella from the stand. "You'd better take this, you'll get soaked out there."

He glanced at her, surprise and puzzlement in his expression, and although he refused the proffered umbrella he muttered something she couldn't catch, opened the stout door, and went outside to be swallowed up in the teeming sheets of sleety rain.

She watched him go and her heart cried out to him in an agonised protest. I know how you feel! I know how you feel, Dr Lorn Campbell. I too love someone who has rejected me and the agony is so hard to bear – especially when you're alone.

She shivered in the bite of cold air rushing through the still-open door and slowly she pushed it to and stood leaning against it for some time, knowing that a part of her was out there with a man in torment and the other was in this house, plucking up courage to go in and face the young woman she had come here to nurse – and to befriend – if friendship was at all possible with the spoilt, pampered wife of Dr Lorn Campbell.

Chapter Four

When Lucy got back to the sitting room Clarrissa greeted her warmly enough and bade her sit down. "Tell me about yourself, Lucy Pemberton." It wasn't a request, it was an order. She sat with her eyes closed, the long lashes fanning out over high cheekbones, her beautifully manicured hands moving restlessly on the arms of her wheelchair.

Lucy was conscious of other eyes watching her and she turned her gaze up to the wall above the fireplace to see a portrait of Clarrissa, obviously painted when she was 'blithe as a skylark' as Jessie MacSporran put it: she was in a standing pose, one perfectly shaped leg showing provocatively from the slit in the skirt of a long green dress. Her full mouth was parted in a wickedly mischievous smile and her lustrous dark eyes glowed in her cameo-like face.

She was breathtaking. No wonder Lorn Campbell worshipped her; any man would. Her mother had been right.

Now she stirred in her chair and Lucy could feel something of her frustration, like a gaudy bird, imprisoned in a cage for all time. "I'm waiting to hear all about you, little Lucy. Have you lost your tongue?"

Lucy came out of her reverie. "I'm sorry, I was dreaming, I was admiring your picture."

Clarrissa followed her gaze and her mouth twisted. "Ah, yes, the days of wine and roses. Oh, I had such fun then, Lucy. I must tell you about it some time. I used to dance all night. Lorn could never keep up with me, but Andrew . . ."

Nora Bruce arrived with the coffee and her daughter took a cup and gulped down the pills left by her husband. "Move the piano stool, Mother," she instructed. "I feel like some music. It's so dull here. Our new little nurse doesn't seem to want to talk about herself and I'm in no mood for a silly all-girls-together evening."

The sarcasm was back in her again and it struck Lucy that it became more obvious whenever she was in the company of her mother. The stool was moved and she manoeuvred her chair in front of the piano. For a few moments she stared straight ahead, apparently lost in a trance, then her long fingers touched the keys, carressing them, savouring the feel of them before she began to play.

The haunting strains of Beethoven's 'Moonlight Sonata' filled the room. Her touch was sure yet light as thistle-down. She was putting everything into the music and it was as if her very soul soared free with the melody. Lucy had never experienced anything like it. A shiver ran through her, the hairs on the back of her neck stood out. The music tantalised her emotions and evoked in her a feeling of such poignancy that she wanted to sit there and let the tears spill unchecked down her face.

It was a strange, ecstatic, almost unearthly experience to sit there, in that exquisite room, with Clarrissa swaying at the piano; Clarrissa's picture gazing down at her; Clarrissa's presence filling every space; all embracing; all powerful; all demanding . . . smothering.

She choked and gasped and realised she had been holding her breath. She found herself looking dazedly around her. The room pulsated in those moments, the very walls seeming to beat and ebb, beat and ebb, so that it felt as if there was no other world but this, Clarrissa playing, her hands fluttering like butterflies over the keyboard, her head thrown back so that her throat was arched and her hair tumbling down her back.

Her mother sat in the depths of a plush armchair. Her eyes too were closed and a smile hovered at the corners of her normally compressed mouth. Even Sherry sat by the side of his mistress, his doggy face composed into tranquillity. It was ridiculous – it was – stupendous!

"I heard this with Andrew at the Albert Hall!" Clarrissa tossed over her shoulder. "It was a night I shall never forget!"

The music swelled and grew more intense. Clarrissa was playing the sonata again, from the beginning. She was lost in a world of her own. A huge living heart was beating in the room; beat-beating, lub-dub lub-dub lub-dub . . .

Lucy realised it was her own heart, beating in her head. She felt fatigued beyond measure, drained, sucked dry of all her strength. A wave of dizziness washed over her and she felt she had to get outside for a breath of fresh air. The room was so warm. She had dressed for upstairs temperatures; down here it was stifling.

The music was no longer enchanting; it was a greedy, grasping, living thing, controlled by the girl at the piano. Sweat broke on Lucy's brow and she stood up abruptly – just as Clarrissa gave a final sweeping flourish over the keyboard.

Mrs Bruce was standing also and she was clapping

– clapping as if her daughter was a concert pianist and she was in the audience demanding an encore. Lucy almost expected her to shout for one but instead she said, "Wonderful! Wonderful, darling! You haven't lost your touch – oh, you could have made such a career out of your music. I gave you all the chances because I knew you had the gift. Instead you got married and threw it all away – buried yourself in the country—"

"Oh be quiet, Mother, do!" The colour had washed out of Clarrissa's face, leaving her so pale she looked bloodless. "Come on, I'm exhausted. Get me to bed, please, I'll have my bath in the morning."

"Let me help," offered Lucy.

The older girl whirred up to her. "Tomorrow, Nursie, your duties begin. Tonight is Mother's last chance to see her little girl gets off to beddy byes – but . . ." Her eyes glittered like coals in her white face. "You can come in later and tuck me up – make sure I've got my fluffy toy rabbits in beside me."

The strength was returning to Lucy and she said grimly, "I might just do that, Clarrissa, see you've got your toy rabbits and that little rag doll you call Lucy."

Clarrissa laughed. "Oh, I threw that away years ago, tore it from limb to limb till it was just a bundle of old rags – the way it started." She patted her knee. "Up Sherry, up!" she commanded, and the little golden spaniel jumped up obediently to be borne from the room in style.

Lucy was left alone, the beat of the piano still ringing in her ears. Outside the rain was rushing down through the gutters, the sea boomed and sighed, boomed and sighed, somewhere in that outside world she had barely glimpsed since her arrival. When was that? Hours? Years ago? In that outer world, in another time it seemed, was Allan, so far away from her now in every sense. Out there too was another man, torn like she was by the loneliness of a love that wasn't returned. He had said he would talk to her if she was up when he came home. The thought struck her – how often did he come home, wearily home, to no one to talk to? No one to listen . . .?

The heat of the room was oppressive. Her eyelids grew heavier, she had to get to bed . . . to sleep, to sleep, perchance to dream, she smiled wryly to herself. But all her dreams were broken . . . she had nothing, no one to dream about. . . .

She gave a little start and knew that she had been sleeping but she didn't open her eyes right away for she was aware that someone was standing by the settee looking down at her, and she knew, from a faint aroma of medication, that it was Dr Campbell.

She lay quite still though her heart was racing with the alarm of waking, not in her own familiar room, but in the sitting room of Moorgate House with the doctor standing above her, watching her. She was amazed and startled at the strength of his presence. How long had he been there? And would she have slept on if she hadn't been lifted up and out of slumber by the power of his nearness?

Every nerve in her body jingled and tautened then, as although he made no sound, she sensed that he had moved away. There was a soft tapping sound, a faint rustling, then the aroma of tobacco smoke sifting to her nostrils. Slowly she opened her eyes to look at him and the sight that met her eyes tore her soft heart in two. He was soaked. A dewy moisture lay on his tweed jacket, his hair was plastered against his head with the unruly lock sticking to his brow; his shoulders were hunched forward as he sat, one hand between his knees, the other holding his pipe in a way that suggested utter weariness.

He was staring dejectedly in front of him, his dark eyes seeing . . . nothing. Compassion engulfed her. They were both prisoners of their own bleak thoughts and tragically she knew she could do nothing to help him. She sat up. "I fell asleep, I waited, I – you said you wanted to see me."

He was immediately alert, brisking his shoulders, the veil back in his eyes, the ice in his voice cutting her to the quick. "There was no need to sit up for me, Miss Pemberton. Go upstairs now, we'll talk in the morning."

"No," she struggled up. "Let me get you a hot drink, you're soaked through, I told you to take the umbrella. . . ."

"Don't concern yourself over me, Miss Pemberton." His tone was peremptory. "I'm quite used to looking after myself and able enough to do so."

Her golden head tilted with pride. "Very well, Doctor, as you say, however, I feel you should put me in the picture about your wife. If I am to do my job efficiently there are certain things I must know."

"Of course, you're right." He tapped out his pipe on the grate and didn't look at her as he went on, "You have met Clarrissa and no doubt have formed some opinions of your own. You have also met my mother-in-law and will have noticed how my wife relies very much on her. . . . Miss Pemberton . . ." his brown eyes looked directly into hers, "that is the reason I have brought you here. Clarrissa has come to depend far too much on her mother. I feel she needs someone younger – someone strong . . ." He hesitated and his glance held hers for a long moment. "The references you sent me are excellent. I see that your last post was in London looking after an old lady and that she thought very highly of you – but – I feel you are a very shy person."

Her face flared crimson and he went on quickly, "You also have spirit; you proved that this evening at dinner." A warmth diffused the steel in his eyes. "Clarrissa needs to meet her match; she likes people to stand up to her. The other young women I employed were never able to do that, and I . . ." Colour touched his own face and he looked down at his hands. "I have never been able to do it either. I give in to her every wish. I shouldn't, it's weak and wrong – but with her – well, she's very strong-willed and if I were to dig in my heels all the time we would never be done arguing. . . ."

He stopped, unable to go on and Lucy had to repress an urge to walk over to him and reassure him with a comforting touch. But he was angry at himself for having allowed his mask to slip and his voice was flat as he continued. "You must be very firm with her and I hope to God, for all our sakes, you will, in time, become – if not soulmates – at least friends. I – think you should also know that her ailment cannot be traced to any real physical cause. . . .'

He paused again, remembering Clarrissa as she had once been: so vibrantly alive, never still for a moment, like a butterfly, restlessly flitting from one bright attraction to the next. Once she had filled his vision with her light, but she had never fully returned his love, and gradually his own had faded to be replaced by other feelings; some affection certainly, he could never forget what she had once been to him. But mostly nowadays, he was motivated by a sense of duty towards her, born out of feelings of guilt for what had happened to her. She had blamed him for getting her pregnant and, afterwards, for losing the baby,

33

as if it had been his hand that had pushed her downstairs on that dreadful night she had tripped and fallen and had gone into premature labour. . . .

He became aware that Lucy was watching him, waiting for him to go on, and taking a deep breath he said flatly, "She has been examined by one doctor after another and they have all come to the same conclusion – that her disability can only be referred to as a functional disorder, psychosomatic if you like – originating from a deep-seated emotional trauma.

"When she lost the baby after falling downstairs, she blamed everything on that, and that is all I am able to tell you at this stage. There are some things that I can't bring myself to talk about yet. It is enough that you should know she is a very emotional person and has a temperament which swings from one mood to another without warning. She is easily aroused to temper and has to have tranquillisers to calm her. Twice since the onset of her disability she has attempted to take an overdose of drugs and now I have to supervise all medication. My surgery and dispensary are at the end of the hall, in a separate extension, and only I have the key.

"Do you think you can handle the situation, Miss Pemberton? Clarrissa may be difficult enough but more trying still will be the opposition you will receive from her mother. Nora had ambitions for her daughter; marrying a country doctor was not one of them, however, and she is highly resentful of me for having had the audacity to appear on the scene and . . ." he smiled wryly, "whisk her daughter away to a life of near-oblivion in the wilds of Scotland! In a sense you will be taking on both Clarrissa and her mother. The task is not an easy one," he finished softly.

"I've had to deal with worse, Doctor," Lucy told him with a conviction she was far from feeling. She looked straight into his eyes. "I'll do everything in my power to help your wife, though you have just hinted there are certain things you do not wish to discuss with me. You have every right to keep your personal matters to yourself, though I hope in time you might feel you can trust me enough to give me some further details about the things that have affected her mind so deeply. Until I get a clearer picture of everything that's involved in her case I feel that any involvement I have with her will be of a limited nature."

She got up and walked over the thick cream-coloured carpet to the door. His voice stayed her. "I hope you'll be happy here. We do have some light with the shade. The folk in this part are friendly and will soon make you feel at home." His voice was low, the musical burr of it so pleasing she could have listened to it forever without wearying.

"Thank you, Doctor, and goodnight," she said, equally quietly, and went out to the wood-panelled hall where a grandfather clock lazily tick-tocked the minutes away. She was surprised to see that it was only yet eleven o'clock and she wondered if she ought to look in on Clarrissa. But then she realised that she didn't know where the bedroom of that young woman lay and slowly she moved to the foot of the stairs and went up to her room.

She was in bed and almost asleep when a board creaked in the corridor and the soft tread of footsteps passed her room. A door squeaked faintly then there was silence and she knew, with only a faint touch of surprise, it was the man she had just left. Clarrissa, beautiful Clarrissa, slept alone downstairs, surrounded no doubt with opulent luxuries. Next door slept her mother – and, banished upstairs like a naughty child, her husband spent his solitary night hours.

Lucy closed her eyes and drifted. She felt unreal. Here she was, in a house that had been an unknown element in her life only that morning. The names of the occupants had just been black markings on pieces of paper. Now, in a matter of a few hours, they were all people in whose lives she was already becoming involved. It was a web, a tangled web, and in the centre was a big fat spider with several victims paralysed and neatly wrapped, ready to be devoured when the time was ripe.

She was at the edge, crawling in . . . and the spider was waiting, waiting. . . . But who was the predator who waited and watched? Who was the one who sapped the very marrow out of living souls? She stirred. She was drifting, dreaming, almost asleep – and for the first time in weeks she was too tired even to cry over Allan.

Chapter Five

Lucy soon discovered that the entire lower half of Moorgate House had been adapted to suit Clarrissa, even the kitchen, though it was doubtful if she spent much time in there. Breakfast was served by Nora Bruce in the kitchen. A tray had been laid for Clarrissa. "I'll take it through to her," said Lucy firmly, and she went up the hall to a door on the left.

Clarrissa was sitting up in bed surrounded by satin cushions. The room was big and light with pale pink carpeting and white furnishings. French windows opened onto a terrace and green lawns. Beyond, the sea sparkled in a sun which was gently lifting the gossamer mist clinging to distant blue hills. The rain of the night before had left everything fresh and the morning world looked newly washed.

Lucy felt her heart lifting with pleasure. It was a beautiful part of Scotland. From her own bedroom she had glimpsed heather moors stretching to the right and left of her, gently rising to the hills. The view of the sea was unparalleled and she had spied a tiny cove nestling among rocks, reached by the lawns.

She greeted Clarrissa cheerily and set the tray on a folding breakfast table. Sherry was sprawled across the satin cushions but sat up eagerly as the smell of bacon reached his nose.

"Don't worry, Sherry, darling, you'll get most of it," sighed his mistress wearily. "I'm not in the least hungry."

"I'm not surprised," Lucy remarked with a little frown. "This room is like an oven. You need some air to give you an appetite. We'll go out after you've had your bath."

Clarrissa looked genuinely shocked. "Out! But, it's December . . ."

"Yes, it's December and the sun is shining. You ought to get some colour into your cheeks."

"Oh, don't be so nursie Nursie," said Clarrissa petulantly. "I never go out in winter and I've no intention of starting now."

"Clarrissa, you may not have the use of your legs but you can see, hear . . . and — and breathe — and it's time you stopped behaving like a dying old woman. I'll be along in half an hour to get you up." She shut the door on a high-pitched indignant yell of outrage and stood for a minute till her heart returned to something near its normal beat then she went back up the hall to the kitchen.

Dr Campbell had just come in and she remembered that she had heard the phone ringing in his room in the early hours of morning. Through the mists of sleep she was aware that outside her room the floorboard had creaked and that soft footsteps went on and down the stairs. He had been called out in the middle of the night and looked pale and drawn. Also, she noted he was coughing.

He gave a slight nod to acknowledge her entry then went on with his breakfast. The kitchen was flooded with sunshine. With the coming of day Moorgate House had taken on an entirely different aspect and she was longing to explore the grounds. "I'm taking Clarrissa out this morning," she announced, buttering her toast with careful deliberation.

Nora Bruce's fork stopped in midair. "Oh, c'mon, my dear child, don't be silly!" she scoffed. "Clarrissa never goes out in such cold weather. The climate here has never been good for her."

Lucy's chin set in the determined lines that Dr Campbell, sitting opposite, was already beginning to know and admire. Lucy had wakened that morning full of doubts over the role she was to play in the household for she knew that Nora Bruce might be a greater challenge to her than the girl she had come to nurse. Then she had thought of Allan, how he had lied and cheated, taken advantage of her youth and naivety. She vowed then that no one else, whether male or female, would do so again. She was going to succeed in this new life and no one, not even Mrs Bruce, was going to stop her.

Looking out at the sea and moors, her resolve had been further strengthened. Daylight had brought normality to the house, had put things into a clearer perspective, and she told herself that its occupants were, after all, just people with the same sort of problems that might be encountered in any household in the land.

"Your daughter needs fresh air, Mrs Bruce," she said firmly. "As a nurse I feel I know best how to cope with her health and I fully intend to see that she gets out. She is a young woman after all, and quite able to contend with a bit of fresh air."

An angry red burned high on the older woman's cheeks but she said nothing more on the subject. The doctor let a few minutes elapse before he asked, "Can you drive a car, Miss Pemberton?"

"Of course I can, Dr Campbell, I started taking lessons as soon as I was old enough to learn."

"Grand, just grand!" he sounded jubilant. "I had a car specially adapted for my wife but she seldom uses it. The manual controls can still be operated and I would be grateful if you would take her out now and then – go for drives – or even take an occasional trip to Campbeltown. There are one or two shops there and Clarrissa was always fond of window-gazing."

"I would be delighted to do that, Dr Campbell," said Lucy and she rose from the table.

He too stood up, looking at his watch. "Nearly nine; time for morning surgery."

He accompanied her up the hall and stopped at a door at the top. "This leads to the extension which I use for my surgery and dispensary," he explained in a low voice. "The patients come in by an outer door so that we can be private here in the house. If you ever need any pills or the like for Clarrissa, tell me and I'll get them for you."

He left her abruptly, but she could hear his rasping cough on the other side of the door and she guessed he had caught a chill from his soaking of the previous night.

It was an easy enough matter getting Clarrissa into the bath using a pulley with a canvas sling attachment. Her body was beautiful, if a little thin, but Lucy felt a catch in her throat seeing the once-perfect legs now rather wasted.

Clarrissa saw her looking and the petulant mouth twisted. "Not a pretty sight, are they, Nursie? They used to look like a million dollars and men couldn't keep their eyes off them. Now they turn away from me as if I was some sort of monster from outer space they daren't look at in case they get smitten. You do know,

I suppose, about me falling downstairs and giving birth to a pitifully premature little baby? I never really wanted one in the first place, but I think Lorn saw it as a means of giving me something to do to keep me occupied.

"It was all so horrid, I shall never get over it – and of course, I ended up being paralysed from a combination of the tumble I took and the dreadful things they did to me in hospital. Oh, I hate it all so, I feel so helpless, having to rely on other people to do everything for me."

Lucy gazed thoughtfully at the beautiful pouting face in front of her and said casually, "There's a lot you could manage to do on your own, Clarrissa. You're quite a strong person really; your arms are perfect and there's nothing wrong with your hands."

Clarrissa was stunned into silence for a moment but she soon found her tongue: "Why, you cheeky little Yorkshire brat! How dare you tell me what I can and can't do? You're here to do it for me and don't allow yourself to forget that fact for one single moment while you're in this house!"

Lucy coloured a little but managed to say briskly, "Come on, the water's getting cold, and I'm not having you blaming me for that when it's you who's doing all the talking."

Up to her neck in soap bubbles Clarrissa lay back with a blissful sigh and, with a wicked little smile lifting the corners of her mouth, she told Lucy, "I don't feel in the least like going out this morning, Nursie dear, and there's not a thing you can do to make me."

Lucy rubbed her nose with the back of a soapy hand and gave Clarrissa a long considering gaze before saying softly, "Oh, isn't there? What if I were to leave you in the bath till the water gets nice and cold; wait till you promise to behave?"

The older girl's dark eyes grew huge with shock and she spluttered, "How dare you, you pitiful little rag doll! How dare you treat me like a child?"

"Because you behave like one, that's how."

"I'll scream for Mother. Wait till she hears of this!"

"Scream all you like. Your mother has gone out to do some shopping and is then going on to visit a friend so won't be back till lunch time. You can insult, cry, scream, till you're blue in the face, Clarrissa, and it won't do you a bit of good. Now, tell me where you keep your warm jumpers and things and I'll go and fetch them."

To her astonishment Clarrissa gave in almost meekly and in less than twenty minutes they were outside the house, and moving over the sun-drenched lawns to the cove where a grassy slope gave Clarrissa access to the shore.

The panorama of blue sea and sky lay spread out before them; gulls swooped and cried; oystercatchers ran busily in the rock pools; foaming little wavelets rattled the shells on the sands; Sherry sniffed and snuffled joyfully, his golden coat gleaming in the sun; the breeze pranced over the moors and into the cove, ruffling Lucy's naturally curling hair and leaving it just faintly windblown. Clarrissa's thick black waves were lifted and tossed into disarray and angrily she pushed the wilful strands out of her eyes. "I hate the wind!" she snapped crossly. "And it's damned-well freezing out here, Lucy. Get me back to the house this minute."

"Go yourself, you're perfectly capable."

"D'you know, you're a perfect little beast, Lucy

42

Pemberton! I can get down that slope alright but I need a push to get back."

Lucy picked up a stone and hurled it into the water. "In a minute," she said calmly. "I'm enjoying myself. Is that your boat up there?" She pointed to the rocks behind them where a white dinghy lay upturned for the winter.

"It's Lorn's, he does a bit of fishing in the summer when he's got the time. He's always on at me to go out with him but Mother hates the water."

"I thought you said he asked you."

Clarrissa's eyes threw sparks. "Mother doesn't think it's safe for me and she's right. Oh, I long for London, we came from there you know – well, Epsom. We used to go to concerts, theatres, dances. . . . Oh hell, what's the use of telling you, you don't look at all interested. Are you a little country girl? Is that why you're staring at the sea as if you could gulp it all down in one go?"

Lucy couldn't help laughing. "Oh, Clarrissa, you're quite funny in your own way. I am a country girl as a matter of fact. I was brought up on a farm and though I've worked in London I was always homesick for green fields, so I'm delighted to be here in this beautiful place and if you would stop sighing over the past you might start to enjoy it too." Then she added, as if it was an afterthought, 'If you were so keen on the bright city lights, why did you marry Lorn Campbell, knowing he was a country doctor?"

"Why, for the novelty of course," drawled Clarrissa, staring at Lucy in rather a defiant fashion. "He was such a dear and really quite besotted by me and he wasn't one of your poor struggling country GPs. I established that fact quite early on in our relationship or I would never even have entertained the idea of marriage. I'm pretty ruthless you see, Lucy, and I don't mind admitting to it. What's the use of withering away miserably without money when you can wither away comfortably with it? "Anyway, all that is beside the point. I thought it would be such fun being married to Lorn: the dutiful little wife, the country house. I imagined party weekends, the house filled with people, all of them so envious of me and my position."

She gave a short bitter laugh. 'But it didn't work out like that. It was too far for them to come. Only the hardy few crossed the border and only in the summer when it was declared a snow-free zone!

"Oh, perhaps it was wrong of me to marry Lorn; he was never one for bright lights and parties. I thought . . ." her mouth trembled," . . . I could change him, but I couldn't, and now he's bound to me whether he likes it or not. He's a creature of great honour and loyalty. I'm not very nice to him sometimes, I get so bored and frustrated and take it out on him. He should retaliate; it's what I need. But he never does, and that makes me worse.

"One day, I feel, he might snap. I won't be too surprised if he does but oh – why am I telling you all this? You're a stranger here. Yesterday morning I hadn't even met you and now I'm telling you my life story, trusting you with my innermost thoughts. . . ."

She gave an impatient shrug. "Oh, c'mon, get me out of here, my wheels are sinking in the sand!"

Lucy hauled her up the beach but was stopped in her tracks by a yell.

"Oh, look, Sherry's found something – a bird I think."

Lucy went to the rocks where Sherry was dancing around, sniffing at something lying on the ground, and picked up a terrified Eider duck that had become entangled

44

in fishing line wound so tightly round its neck it was in danger of strangulation.

Clarrissa held out her hands and gently took the golden brown bundle from Lucy. "The poor little thing!" she cried, her voice full of compassion. "Perhaps Lorn can fix it up. Let's take it back to the house."

The bird snuggled against her and Lucy said softly, "You wouldn't find the likes of that in the streets of London, Clarrissa, the country has its compensations."

The older girl looked at her and though she said nothing, a strange expression had crept into her eyes and Lucy knew she had touched a chord in the heart of a city girl who loved animals.

Chapter Six

Lorn expertly removed the line from the bird's neck and Clarissa took the creature in her arms once more. "Poor little Eider," she crooned. "You shall come with me to my room and we shall rest together . . . I'm so tired."

She shot an accusing glance at Lucy but there was a hint of colour in her porcelain cheeks, and Lorn looked at Lucy and smiled, a warm slow smile that, as before, transformed a rather serious man into a boy. The sight of his wife's rosy cheeks had obviously pleased him.

Meg Stewart arrived at eleven to start preparing lunch, and over a cosy cup of tea Lucy learned a little more about her employers. She was naturally curious though she hated the idea of gossip, but she soon found that Meg was no scandalmonger; she just talked naturally, without malice, and it soon became obvious to Lucy that she thought the world of Lorn Campbell.

"A fine, fine laddie, that he is," she told Lucy, draining her cup to the dregs before replenishing it from the big brown teapot keeping warm on the hob. "And a grand doctor into the bargain, out in all weathers and never a grumble out of him. My man, Bob, has been a semi-invalid for three years now – his heart you know

– and that laddie never passes our cottage without looking in on my Bob."

She paused, and her honest eyes scrutinised Lucy kindly. "For his sake I hope you stick it here, lassie; all the others left. The girl's mother, she drove them away. Ach, she's an interfering body, that she is. If she left the lass alone with her man they might be able to sort things out for themselves – but no – like a leach she is – and putting the lass against her own man – blaming him for everything. Has anyone told you yet what happened?"

Lucy shook her head. "Only bits here and there. I've been trying to piece it all together. I know that Clarrissa fell downstairs, which brought on the birth of a stillborn baby – a year ago I think."

"Ay," Meg nodded slowly and sadly. "The wee mite, premature it was, a son. She had an epidural for the birth and afterwards she said she couldn't walk. The doctors said no nerve damage had been done but she was never convinced of that and hasn't moved a muscle since, saying it was a combination of the fall and the things that happened to her in hospital."

Meg's homely face grew sadder as she went on, "Nora Bruce had big plans for her daughter's future; she gave her a good education and Clarrissa ended up going to music college and coming out with all sorts of honours and degrees. But she was too fond of enjoying herself to really take her future seriously, much to her mother's dismay.

"She kept on hoping that her daughter would return to her studies, or marry a man with some social status, preferably someone in the sort of limelight that Clarrissa could share. Then Lorn appeared in her life. He met the girl in London four years ago when he was having a

47

wee holiday like. Ach, he never was a lad for the cities but his brother was away abroad for a few months and it was a good chance to make use of the flat.

"He met Clarrissa and lost his head over her, but my, she kept him on a string; made the soul suffer till she was ready. And by God! she knew a good thing when she saw it but didn't want him to know what a good catch he was. For two months he ran back and forth to London before she finally agreed to marry him. And the fuss that Mrs Bruce made about the wedding! You would have thought it was royalty going to the altar. She made a good hole in Lorn's pocket right from the start and it's never stopped since. Want, want, want; take, take, take; and for all the poor soul gets in return."

Lucy's hands tightened on her cup. She felt unaccountably sad and her heart went out to Lorn Campbell. Were these the reasons his manner to her was so icily distant? Did he mistrust all women? Think that they were all as malicious and hurtful as Mrs Bruce – and Clarrissa?

But something told her Clarrissa was not like her mother. She was vain, pampered, selfish, but there was also a softness in her that was lacking in her mother. Lucy had witnessed it that morning in the cove with the injured bird. If she could show such compassion to a wounded creature, why couldn't she show it to her husband, the man she must once have loved, the man whose child she had borne? Why did she allow her mother to drive a wedge between herself and the hurt, lonely man who walked alone, fought his lonely fight alone, bore the brunt of the blame for Clarrissa's tragic illness alone?

Well, he wasn't alone now. She was here, and she would help him in the battle with the woman who had

48

come into his home to hammer the wedge between him and Clarrissa a little deeper every day.

With a sigh Meg rose and said, "Now, if it had been Andrew, Mrs Bruce would have patted his head and told him it wasn't his fault, but there you are, it's the way of things . . . Mercy! Would you look at the time, and me with the vegetables yet to prepare!"

Andrew! Lucy frowned. It was the third time that name had cropped up. Last night Clarrissa had said it, her dark eyes dreamily distant as her lips had formed the word 'Andrew' almost reverently.

By dinner time that evening Lorn Campbell's cough was much worse. Lucy saw that he was fevered, with a spot of red burning high on the cheekbones of his thin, tired face, but when she suggested that he ought to get an early night he turned on her fiercely and as much as told her to mind her own business. His evening surgery had been packed out and he hadn't got through till almost seven-thirty so that he barely had time to sit back and relax before dinner.

He had no appetite that evening. The unruly lock of his hair clung damply to his sweating brow and he was shivering.

"Lorn, dear, Nursie is right for once," said Clarrissa, and Lucy thought again how changed she was in her mother's presence. "You really ought to get up to bed. I can't bear to hear anyone coughing, it goes for my nerves."

"I quite agree." Nora Bruce didn't look up. "I always think it's so unfair of people to go spreading their germs about then have the cheek to turn round and call it bravery. Clarrissa mustn't be exposed to these nasty things you catch from your patients. Go up to bed, there's a dear."

Her voice was flat, with no trace of sympathy. Lucy felt like slapping her. The woman was impossibly hard-hearted. Lorn got up without a word but at the door he turned. "Goodnight, Clarrissa. At least you're looking the better for your outing today."

Nora Bruce snorted and Clarrissa laughed. "The cold almost killed me. I shan't go out again and that's a promise – by the way, Lorn, dear, don't forget to leave out my pills, I've been a good girl today, did everything Nursie told me so I think I deserve a reward."

He turned away and looked so lost and full of a desolate despair that Lucy couldn't stop a cry of protest. "Wait – Doctor! Do you have an electric blanket? You can't go into a cold bed."

He didn't turn round and his back bristled with resentment. "No, Miss Pemberton, I do *not* have an electric blanket and I do not *need* an electric blanket."

Meg's voice floated from the kitchen. "Ach, he's stubborn – just like my Bob. I'll fill a couple of hot water bottles and you put them in his bed, lassie."

"I'll do that." Lucy was on her high horse now. "And I'll bring you up a hot drink, Doctor."

"Nursie will make it better." Clarrissa's voice came low but clear, but Lucy didn't deign to answer. Instead she got up and went through to the kitchen where a sparkling-eyed Meg thrust the hot bottles into her hands.

"That's good, lassie," she whispered delightedly. "You tell them, and see that boy gets some attention. I'll make a jug of cocoa and leave it here by the stove – and a wee hot toddy wouldn't go amiss either."

"Toddy?"

50

"Ay, a dram of whisky topped up with hot water and sweetened with honey. Finest cure-all for 'flu and the like."

Lucy's eyes gleamed. "I know what you mean, my dad makes himself a brew like that when he's got a cold, and swears by it."

She made her way upstairs to the doctor's room. At a glance she saw that though it was clean there were traces of masculine untidiness, and it lacked little touches of comfort such as only a wife or mother might provide.

She rolled his pyjama top round one bottle and was carrying out a similar procedure with the bottoms when he came into the room to stand behind her and watch in silence. His rasping breathing filled the room and she said without looking at him. "Give me the keys to the surgery and I'll get you some cough mixture from the dispensary."

Still he said nothing, but when she turned she saw a look in his eyes she couldn't fathom: puzzlement, bewilderment, she didn't know, but obediently he took the keys from his pocket and gave them to her.

When she got back with a tray containing the jug of cocoa, a glass of toddy and a bottle of cough mixture, he was in bed, lying very still, gazing up at the ceiling. When she put the tray down on his jumbled bedside cabinet he looked at it and a smile curved his sensitive mouth. "God, you're efficient, aren't you? I thought only mothers did such things."

"Did yours?"

"Ay," he murmured, "she did, here in this very room when I was a wee boy. She used to rub my chest with Vick and help me over my ails. Too bad I couldn't do the same for her when she was

51

ill and me all grown up and a doctor into the bargain."

"She sounds just like my mother," said Lucy briefly, a sadness in her that his mother was no longer around to 'cure his ails'. Silently she stood by while he drank the toddy and gulped down some cough mixture. She was bending over, straightening the covers, when his hand came out and took hers in a grip that made her wince. The heat of him burned into her, but more than that she was aware that a sensation like an electric shock had passed from his body through hers.

"Thank you," he said huskily, and she thought she saw the bright gleam of tears in the dark mesh of his long lashes. She was surprised to feel that her heart was beating rapidly, and the touch of his hand so moved her she drew hers away quickly.

The veil came back over his brown eyes once more, and he lay back, breathing heavily. "You're here to try and mend a broken heart, aren't you, Miss Pemberton?"

She gasped as he went on, "I'm an expert on such matters. I can feel the same pain in you that once tore me apart. It will go, Miss Pemberton, believe me, in time it will go – but – don't let bitterness take its place – it would be a pity in one so—" He stopped abruptly and turned his head away from her so that his eyes were hidden from her. "Go now and see to Clarrissa – and keep up the good work you started today – she needs someone to tell her what to do."

She left him lying in the softly-lit room. Feeling strangely shaken she stood for some time in the passageway – wondering – wondering why it was that the nearness of a man she had known little more than twenty-four hours disturbed her so greatly. She decided it must be compassion she felt, that and the fact that they both shared a common grief, and she braced her shoulders and went downstairs.

All night long she knew he tossed and turned, for every time she awoke she heard him rasping and coughing. It must have been about five-thirty when she wakened to hear the phone ringing insistently in his room. It was very cold in that chill hour of morning. An icy blast of sea air billowed her curtains and, shivering, she got up to shut her window, hopping from rug to rug so that her feet wouldn't touch the cold wooden floor.

The phone had stopped now, and with a shock she realised he must have answered it; it hadn't rung long enough for the person on the other end of the line to give up trying. Common sense told her that the only thing he could do was answer a call from a patient, but it was up to her to see that he wasn't going to be fool enough to get up out of his bed.

Quickly she pushed her feet into slippers, donned a dressing-gown, and went out of her room and up the corridor to tap on his door. There was no response, and with a boldness she was far from feeling she turned the knob and went in.

He was struggling out of bed. She saw that his pyjamas were soaked in perspiration and his face flushed with fever. "You're surely not going out?" she cried at him.

"For God's sake, will you leave me alone, girl! Who the hell do you think you are, coming into this house and ordering us all about?"

"It looks as if it's time somebody did some ordering!" she yelled back. "Tell me who your locum is and I'll ring him at once."

"The hell you will! Get out of my room and leave me alone. I'm a doctor, dammit, and I've got a job to do!"

"And I'm a nurse with a job to do and by God I'm going to do it while there's breath in me. I've been given the task of dealing with your spoilt wife, and also have to take a lot of aggravation from her equally spoiled mother, but I'm damned if I'm going to be insulted by a doctor who behaves like a baby! It seems to me it's time *everyone* in this place grew up!"

For a long minute they glared at each other, then, quite suddenly he sank back into his pillows and indicated the note pad at his bedside. "Dr Millar. His number's in there."

She picked up the phone. "I'll ask him to go out to the patient who just called – then I want him to come round here and see you."

The smooth skin on his face went a shade brighter. "Miss Pemberton, don't you dare!" But she was already explaining matters to Dr Millar, though when she put the phone down she didn't dare glance at the outraged figure in the bed.

"I'll get you a cup of tea and you can have some more of that mixture," she told him.

On her way downstairs the funny side of the incident struck her and she put her hand to her mouth to smother a burst of laughter. He could gladly have hit her up there in the bedroom. No wonder. She had called him a baby and the recollection chased away her laughter and made her wonder instead at her own audacity. If only Mum and Dad could have heard it all they would have told her she was more like her old self.

She stopped in the act of filling the kettle. Was she? But how could she be? Last night she had dreamed of

Allan. He had beckoned to her from a gossamer curtain and when she glided through it she saw his bronzed body dressed only in swimming briefs. In slow motion she had gone to take his outstretched hand and they had run over hot sands into the sea. It was warm. They stood up to their waists in the water and his blue eyes were bluer than the sky. Without any conscious effort or obvious movement she melted into his arms and his lips were kissing her ears, her throat, her mouth.

His kisses became more demanding, probing, his hands were moving over her breasts, gliding down to her thighs, pulling her in closer to his body which was taut with urgency. A core of fire burned deep inside her body; she was trembling with a need to let the flames spread outwards, downwards, but when he was at his most insistent, pulling her in towards him under the silken water, she gave a little cry of protest and pushed him away and he was left, his arms outstretched in appeal. But she shook her head and told him "No", and then he had looked at her with disgust, and had floated away from her to be lost in the nebulous curtain.

"Allan, Allan, darling, don't go!" She had cried out and had awakened saying his name over and over, her face and pillow wet with tears. She wondered if Lorn Campbell had heard her tossing and crying in her dreams, and felt oddly disturbed that he should.

Dr Millar arrived just after six-fifteen. He was a bald, bespectacled little man who was completely unruffled at being called out of bed at such an hour.

"Nurse Pemberton was quite right to call me," he told an embarrassed Lorn Campbell. "Glad to see someone in the house with a bit of sense at last. You've got a bad dose of 'flu, Lorn, and the beginnings of bronchitis into the bargain. You'll have to stay in bed for a few days. I'll give you some antibiotics. That should clear up your chest."

"But the place is jumping with chills and 'flu, John, I ought to be up, seeing to it," groaned the younger man.

"You'll do no such thing, my boy. I'm quite well able to take over for a while." His eyes twinkled behind his glasses. "I've still got one foot and a leg outside the grave you know and I quite enjoy keeping my hand in the old medicine barrel." He winked. "I haven't heard a good bit of juicy gossip for a long time so I'll come over at nine and see to morning surgery. Lie back and enjoy a good rest – you work too damned hard anyway."

Lucy appeared tentatively in the doorway. Her curls were a ruffle of gold about her heart-shaped face and her deep blue-grey eyes were wary, as if she didn't relish the outcome of her hasty decision-making earlier.

She was still attired in her pink towelling robe and looked so naturally attractive that Dr Millar's eyes swept over her approvingly. "Beauty as well as brains! You've certainly landed lucky, Lorn my lad."

He got up, and going to the door, surreptitiously took Lucy's arm and led her out to the passageway. "He's exhausted as well as ill, my lassie," he told her seriously. "Are you up to nursing him as well as Mrs Campbell for a few days?"

"I can certainly do my best, Dr Millar."

He patted her arm kindly. "Good girl. I'll be along later and will take a look in on him again." He paused at the top of the stairs and his approving look was on her again. "You've got what it takes, young woman.

I think you'll make a go of it here." He nodded his bald head and went away muttering, "Indeed, it's time somebody did."

Chapter Seven

Over the next few days Lucy was kept so busy she tumbled exhausted into bed each night and slept soundly till the alarm shrilled her into wakefulness at six o'clock. She found that the sole task of nursing Lorn Campbell was left to her. Nora Bruce would not so much as take a tray up to him and it seemed as if she had started some sort of personal vendetta against Lucy, who would have welcomed a bit of help with Clarrissa, but got none.

Nora Bruce laid dainty trays for her daughter, sat with her in the afternoons and spent the evenings with her in the sitting room, but lift a hand to do anything else she would not. Although Lucy was more tired than she had ever been in her life she did not for one moment let the older woman see it.

Meg stomped happily up to visit Lorn every day, filling his ears with all sorts of chatter and for this Lucy was grateful, for good doctor he might be, but a good patient he was not, and he was bored and irritable lying in his bed. Every day he asked after Clarrissa and once he said to Lucy, "It would be nice to see her running upstairs, wouldn't it?"

He pines for her when he's up here, thought Lucy, and a stab of pain shot through her. Lucky, lucky Clarrissa to be so loved. If only she would return it. If Allan loved me like that . . .

Clarrissa at this point was full of surprises that Lucy never expected. Every day she asked after Lorn. Once she took herself off to the kitchen and prepared a tempting meal for him. She told Lucy, "It's odd: I miss him when he's not around, a bit like Sherry I suppose. If he wasn't here I'd go mad!"

"But – your husband is hardly to be compared to a pet dog, Clarrissa," objected Lucy.

The older girl smiled mischievously. "He is to me, don't you think he's a bit of a pet? Obedient; well trained; trusting; looking at me out of those big golden-brown eyes of his. You know, I believe if I said 'fetch' to him he would do it."

On the third day she demanded angrily, "When are you taking me out again, Lucy? You're supposed to be *my* nurse and companion but you're more like *Lorn's* as far as I can make out."

Lucy gasped. "You said you hated going out!"

"The hell with what I say! It's what I enjoy that matters! We could go out in the car this afternoon – that's if you can spare the time of course."

"I can spare it, Clarrissa," said Lucy and she laughed.

But it was difficult finding enough hours in the day to tend both Clarrissa and her husband to their mutual satisfaction. One was as demanding as the other and grew peeved with Lucy if she didn't give each of them her wholehearted attention.

Clarrissa got her run in the car, and both young women got to know one another a little bit better. Clarrissa seemed genuinely to enjoy Lucy's company and only called her 'Nursie' once. But when Lucy announced that she would

59

have to be getting back to see to Lorn the older woman threw a tantrum and yelled that it was *she* who was supposed to be getting all Lucy's attention, and if Lorn wanted in on the act he could damned well hire someone else to run after him.

When at last Lucy made her way upstairs, after putting the car away and seeing Clarrissa settled for her afternoon nap, Lorn greeted her rather distantly and said that no one had been near him for hours and he might as well be dead and buried for all anyone cared about him.

Lucy knew he was feeling very sorry for himself and made no comment as she put the tray of tea and biscuits she had brought, on the bedside table. "Sit up and drink this," she said briskly, and without ado she took hold of his arm to make him lean forward so that she could plump his pillows.

The heat of his burning flesh beat into her and she felt herself growing still and strange when he turned his head to look directly into her eyes and said, "I'm sorry for being such a baby and snapping at you. It isn't your job to look after me and you would have every right to walk out of here this minute and never come near me again."

Lucy's breath caught in her throat. She wanted to cry out, 'Oh, but I *want* to be near you, Lorn Campbell! I've never wanted anything so much for a long time.' Instead she said, "I could never neglect you like that, I'm – I'm a nurse, remember, and the urge to want to look after people is second nature to me. Drink your tea before it gets cold. I'll have a cup with you and tell you about the outing I had with Clarrissa this afternoon."

As the days wore on, Lucy experienced more and more difficulty being close to Lorn without feeling an overpowering urge to touch him and hold him close in her arms and murmur soothing words of comfort in his ear. He was very vulnerable lying there in bed, wakened and sleeping, flushed and warm, his hair rumpled, pyjamas crumpled, watching her with eyes that gave nothing away but were yet filled with a certain light whenever she came into the room. Because he likewise was finding it very hard to be so near her without touching her. He enjoyed watching her, the way she carried herself, the proud little tilt of her chin, the golden halo of her hair under the light, the shyness in her eyes whenever she glanced at him.

"You're a grand little nurse, Lucy Pemberton," he said once, and she blushed to the roots of her hair because it wasn't *what* he said but the way he said it, his voice low and sweet, and somehow intimate.

Four days after taking to bed Lorn got up to shave and have a bath, and Lucy took the opportunity to change and make the bed. She was punching a pillow into shape when the faint smell of soap came to her nostrils and without turning round she knew he was behind her, standing very close.

A tremor went through her body. She could feel his life forces as if they had passed out of him and were flowing inside herself. Why, she wondered, did his nearness make her feel weak and so idiotically out of control of her senses?

Abruptly she spun round to escape the room but he blocked the way, his intense face so close to her own she could see his jaw tightening; could smell the mingled aroma of toothpaste and shaving cream, and she could see that dimple on his wilful chin, alluring and sweet; so irresistibly tempting. She wanted to kiss it; for him to kiss her.

61

The shock of that knowledge made her gasp, and her eyes to darken. He didn't touch her, just stood looking at her for a long, long eternal moment, his own eyes dark with desire. Then he lifted his hand and briefly touched a lock of her golden hair. "Sunshine," he murmured, in the lilting voice she had grown to love in the last few days. "The sunshine of summer is trapped in your hair to lighten the long days of winter. And your eyes . . ." his voice had grown low and husky, "your eyes are like the sea: grey when you are troubled or angry, blue when you're happy. At this moment they are neither one nor the other − but one day the blue will shine out of them again. Personally, I like the grey of them too . . . Did you know they are flecked with amber? Like seaweed . . ."

His hands were clenched at his sides as if it was taking him all his willpower to keep them there. He smiled slowly and the brown of his eyes was lit with gold, like sunshine slanting into the pools of the forest. "Whenever the weather is too bad to go outside I shall look at your eyes and think of the sea."

With one finger he caressed the soft skin of her face. His wide, sensitive mouth trembled slightly and his lips formed her name soundlessly. "Lucy," he sighed, and she felt her heart fluttering so fast she thought she would faint. Lucy. He had called her Lucy, not the formal-sounding "Miss Pemberton" he had used since her arrival.

He said it again, a little louder now, and the pronunciation of her name in his lilting Highland tongue had never been more beautiful. To her now he was Lorn. She had stopped thinking of him as anything else since she had begun to nurse him. Lorn, Lorn, Lorn. It was the most musical name she had ever heard. It breathed of the sea; the hills; romance; music. "Lorn."

She said it aloud but softly, the way it should always be spoken.

"Miss Pemberton." The unmistakable, high, slightly querulous, voice of Nora Bruce broke into the room like a whiplash, and Lucy jumped away from Lorn guiltily, her face so red she might just have been caught in his arms.

"Yes, Mrs Bruce?" She brought her eyes round to look enquiringly at the older woman and saw on her face an expression of satisfaction, almost as if she was pleased to have found them standing so intimately close. But disappointment was on her face too, and with an odd sense of unease Lucy wondered if it was because she had deliberately come upon them unawares and had hoped to find them embracing.

"Clarissa wants you." The tones were clipped. "Would you believe, she actually wants you to go out with her for a walk."

"I quite believe it, Mrs Bruce," returned Lucy evenly, and she walked with her head high out of the room.

Lorn resumed his duties the following day but at lunch time he came into the kitchen looking worried. "Elspeth has gone down with 'flu now," he said dejectedly. Elspeth was the pleasant young receptionist who also took a lot of work off Lorn's shoulders by helping in the dispensary.

"I can give you a hand if you like," offered Lucy.

"But Clarissa needs you," he reminded her. "It seems that we have all been claiming your attention since the moment you arrived . . ." His words trailed off in an unfinished key and she knew that he didn't want to go on addressing her by her surname but couldn't bring himself to call her by her Christian name in his mother-in-law's hearing.

Nora Bruce put her well-shaped nose in the air at his

words. "Well, I for one certainly have not needed Miss Pemberton and hope I never shall, but if it's of any help to you, Lorn dear, I will supervise Clarrissa's bathing and dressing in the mornings to allow Miss Pemberton time to help out in the surgery. Evenings will be no problem of course: Clarrissa is up and doing then and I will make a point of keeping her amused."

"Thank you, Nora," Lorn replied. But Lucy said nothing. She had the strangest notion that the older woman was throwing her and Lorn together deliberately. It was odd that when her son-in-law had been ill she had allowed Lucy to do everything for him and had not lifted a finger to help with her daughter. Now she was making it easy for Lucy to be working close beside Lorn and Lucy decided she was either trying to overburden her with work so that she would be glad to shake the dust of Moorgate House from her heels, or, she was using her as bait to trap Lorn into doing something she would make sure he would regret bitterly.

"The matter is settled then," Lucy said, even while she decided that not for one moment would she give the woman the slightest reason to cause trouble of any sort.

The following week was a complete joy for her. It was fun to be at the little reception desk getting to know the villagers and giving them the opportunity to get to know her. She was sure many of them turned up out of curiosity but they were such friendly, courteous souls she didn't care.

The minister, red-nosed and snuffling, introduced himself to her in determined tones and was delighted when she told him she had every intention of joining the Ardben kirk.

The following evening an earnest young woman turned up, sound of wind and limb but hell bent on extracting a promise from Lucy to help out with the Sunday school's Christmas Eve Nativity, and could Lucy possibly help, "to organize the bairnies with their singing."

In a flurry of impulsiveness Lucy said she would, but later, bemoaning the fact to Lorn that she was absolutely tone deaf, she was surprised when he threw back his dark head and laughed, his eyes crinkling with delight.

If a smile transformed his face, laughter made it glow. She couldn't help staring at him. It was the first real laughter she had heard from him since her arrival at Moorgate House. "Laughter suits you," she said quietly, feeling a slow radiance washing into her heart just because she was near him, and had made him laugh.

The evening surgery was over and they were in the tiny dispensary together, counting pills into little brown bottles. He turned slowly, serious now, and said, "Is it such a stranger in my life that the sight of it makes you stare?"

"Yes, Lorn, it is, it's the first time I've heard you laughing, really and truly laughing with joy since I came here."

"Joy." He said the word slowly, thoughtfully. "Yes, I think I've felt joy these last few days working with you here, close by me."

They were closer now than when they had stood together in the bedroom and their eyes met and held.

"The sea is blue tonight, Lucy," he whispered. "The grey has lifted since last I looked into your eyes."

No, no, she thought, in anguish. Allan is the one who holds my heart, even though he squeezes the happiness out of it. But Allan wasn't here; Lorn was here, tall, dark, sensitive Lorn. Lorn of the sea and the sky; Lorn of the hills and the moors. His name was like the hush of the waves; the soft beguiling cry of a solitary sea bird.

Lorn: living, pulsing, beating, lifting her spirit to the stars. Warm, sweet, Lorn of the lilting Highland voice that washed into her soul like the liquid cry of the curlew.

His fingers curled over her wrist. Those long, beautiful fingers were touching her, and she felt herself drawing nearer to him. His mouth was close and she could feel the warmth of his lips even before they met hers. Now he was kissing her closed lids, her brow, her ears. A tingle ran down the back of her neck to the base of her spine and she gave a little cry and pulled his head down.

His mouth was hard on hers, his tongue pushing, seeking. A whimpering moan came from her throat and they went wild for moments that locked them in an intimate world that was theirs and theirs alone.

His arms were strong around her, embracing her hard into his body. He was demanding and harsh, his kisses so deep they bruised her mouth, but she was beyond caring. "Lucy, Lucy," he breathed. "Sweet, darling, Lucy."

Her fingers curled into the hair at the nape of his neck, her lips moved over his face, and now she was kissing that dimple, that endearing little dimple that had entranced her from the moment she saw it.

He was trembling, carried away by his passions. The tips of his fingers were tracing the fine bones at the top of her spine, then his hand came round to her neck to savour the warm smoothness of her skin. The core of fire inside her body was fanning out till her entire being was diffused with warmth.

His fingers moved to her breasts to stroke the nipples

and she arched her neck, willing to let him do anything – as she had never been with Allan!

In a daze she forced herself out of his arms. If Nora Bruce had come in and found them . . . It was beyond thinking about. Oh God! What was she doing? What was *he* doing? They were playing with fire, driven together by a common need for comfort. It was Clarrissa he loved – no, worshipped – but Clarrissa didn't love *him*, wouldn't let him share her bed since the tragedy of their child's birth. . . .

She struggled out of his arms, panting, gasping on the tears that choked her. "No, Lorn, no, please. It's wrong."

His brown eyes were glazed and far away and he put both hands on the table to lean on it while he fought to regain control of his senses. "I'm sorry," he said, at last. The hardness was back in his voice, and it caught her like a blow. "It won't happen again, I promise you."

He straightened and lifted his head. "I almost forgot: you're still in love with another – it will be better if we aren't alone like this again. Until Elspeth comes back, any work we have to do in the surgery or dispensary will be done alone."

His fingers fluttered aimlessly over the jumble of bottles on the table. "Leave these till morning; it must be almost time for dinner." He strode quickly out of the room leaving her to straighten her clothing with shaking hands.

She glanced through the door to the surgery. He was at his desk, his face in shadow from the angle-poise lamp. He didn't once glance in her direction as she emerged from the dispensary to stand in the doorway, but walked away through the little passage between the reception desk

67

and waiting room and out of the door leading to the hall. He might have been a million miles from her and in the darkness of the waiting room she felt tears pricking her eyelids and she wondered if she would ever be free of the memory of Allan Graham. Whatever she did she mustn't be caught on the rebound. She would not let herself be tempted again, by Lorn Campbell or any other man.

Chapter Eight

She stuck firmly to her resolution till the coming of Andrew into her life at Moorgate House. . . .

It was just a few days before Christmas. The snow was falling gently, draping the hills in sheets of dazzling white, spreading over the countryside in feathery billows that clung to naked branches, dressing them in soft coats that took away the starkness of winter tracery.

The mornings were misty and hoary with frost that clung to fragile stems and grasses and were so beautiful in all their precarious delicacy that Lucy rose early each morning to go outside and scrunch through ice-glittered snow before the sun came up and melted away the brittleness of dawn.

At the back of the house, where the air was laden with salt, the snow soon melted, but the front lawns were virginal, and Clarrissa stunned everyone one day at lunch time by declaring that the thing she wanted most in the world was to go outside and build a snowman. Lucy felt such a great satisfaction at this request that her face glowed and Lorn, looking at her, felt that he had never known what unselfishness was till the coming of this lovely girl into his home.

Casting his mind back he tried to remember what it had been like at Moorgate House without her but it was somehow difficult to do so. She had brought light and life into his home, combined with a warmth that had been lacking for so long.

Recalling the intimacies they had shared in the dispensary his face grew hot and his heart began to beat a little faster. Ever since then he had tried to distance himself from her and was finding it very hard to do so. When he thought she wasn't looking he observed her every move and now knew every shy glance, each little gesture she made. The sound of her light quick footsteps made his pulses race, the sight of her each morning brought a strange sad longing to the very core of his heart. When she smiled at him he wanted to take her in his arms and dance with her around the room, when her mouth trembled he longed to kiss it and soothe away the things that were troubling her.

He knew that she had come to his house in this remote part of Scotland to try and mend a broken heart. All the signs were there; he knew them well, he had suffered the very same symptoms when he had tried so hard to please his wife and show her how much he loved her.

She hadn't wanted him though; he doubted if she ever really had. He had been something of a novelty for her in the beginning, and then she had become bored by him and had hankered after her old way of life, making him miserable in the process, dulling his love for her, turning him into a much harder person than once he had been.

That was one of the reasons he behaved towards Lucy as he did. He didn't want to be hurt again, he never wanted to know that raw ache of pining for someone who couldn't love him for what he was.

He glanced from Lucy to Clarrissa and saw a very changed young woman from the one who had whined and complained incessantly before the coming of Lucy into her life. There was a delicate sparkle of colour in her face; her eyes were alight with a renewed interest in life; she was less bitter and bitchy; no longer did she take to her bed for the least excuse; each morning she arose with alacrity and wanted to know what the weather was like so that she could get out in her chair.

Her appetite had improved to a marked degree, earning her nods of approval from Meg who always liked to see 'a clean plate'. She demanded less tranquillisers and sleeping tablets, and all things considered, she was moving towards a contentment of spirit that gave her an altogether more serene quality of life.

Where Lorn was concerned, she had become more considerate and was thoughtful about his welfare in a careless sort of way, as if she didn't want to let him see that she was in any way retracting her claws too soon.

She still nursed grievances, of that there was no doubt, and he also knew that she would never completely lose her sharpness of tongue; that was something that was inbuilt in her, a part of her make-up that she had inherited from her mother.

The bitch in Clarrissa manifested itself in different ways: she enjoyed tormenting him when she felt like it, and when last night, he had gone to her room to bid her goodnight she had held out her arms to him enticingly, her eyes half-shut like a sleepy cat.

She had been wearing a flimsy nightdress with a long low front opening, and the creamy cleavage of her breasts had become more temptingly voluptuous with the raising of her arms.

He had gone to her without a word and she had taken his dark head in her hands to look for a long time into

71

his eyes before saying, "My poor Lorn, how do you put up with it, I wonder?"

She had kissed him gently then and had pushed his head down to the softness of her breasts. Her skin had been fragrant with a texture like silk. Oh, how she had driven him crazy with that gorgeous body of hers!

At one time in his life she was all he could think about. She had filled his entire vision. He had been consumed by a burning desire that had caused him endless nights of torture, so that at one point he was physically ill with the longing for her. For she had teased him all the time by flirting with other men.

The agony had gone on for quite some time before she had finally relented and said she would marry him, and oh! the ecstasy of possessing her body, of fighting her wild passion with his till finally merging with her in matings that were almost savage.

Lying against her last night, the familiar ache had grown inside him. She had teased him till he could contain himself no longer and had started to make love to her. But he could do nothing to rouse her and in the end he had turned away from her and she had said with the soft mocking laugh he knew so well, "That's what you did to me, Lorn – when you made me have that baby. I feel nothing inside; the lower half of my body doesn't exist for me. This is your punishment, Lorn . . . and the result of your so-called precious love for me."

"Clarrissa!" he had exclaimed in protest, "I didn't do it deliberately, it was just something that – happened."

"Oh, did it?" she had retaliated bitterly. "You could have been more careful but you were too selfish. Mother's right: men are selfish beasts. Oh, go away! I can't stand to look at you at this moment."

She had turned her face into her satin pillows and had begun to weep, and he had known it was useless to attempt to comfort her when she was in such a mood.

But this morning she was bright again and talking about going outside to play in the snow. She was like a little girl in her eagerness and Lucy smiled, but couldn't look at Lorn. He had hurt her deeply by almost ignoring her existence since that night in the surgery. She hardly saw him except at mealtimes. When he wasn't working he made a point of always having some excuse for not being in the same room as she. Every night after dinner he disappeared back to his desk in the surgery with the pretence of studying.

She immersed herself into her job and in the affairs of the village, and, was surprised to wake up one morning to the realisation that she hadn't cried for Allan for some time.

After lunch she and Clarrissa spent a joyous afternoon in the snow and amazingly, Nora Bruce, suitably dressed in a padded anorak and good sensible boots, came out to join in the fun, though Lucy would have preferred it if she hadn't taken part, for her very presence gave more than the usual spice to Clarrissa's tongue. Once or twice she called Lucy "Nursie" and threw her mother a sly sidelong glance as if savouring the reciprocal note of approval.

It hadn't really mattered though; the three women had thoroughly enjoyed themselves playing in the snow. Clarissa had shrieked like an excited child, Lucy had pelted her with snowballs, and Nora Bruce had surprised both Clarrissa and Lucy by declaring herself to be as hungry as a hunter and going indoors to make mugs of piping hot cocoa for everyone, supplemented with thick wedges of oven-fresh apple tart.

After tea Lucy put on her thick jacket and boots and went down the driveway of Moorgate House to walk the half-mile to Ardben kirk for a rehearsal with the Sunday school. The tiny kirk of Ardben was a sturdy, century-old building of grey, weathered stone which time and nature had blotched with orange and yellow lichens.

In the old part of the graveyard, ancient bones lay mouldering under mounds of tough grass, overshadowed by moss and ivy-covered headstones bearing spidery writings about generations long gone.

The newer cemetery sloped towards the sea and was sheltered from the elements by groves of oak and sycamore that made it look protected and less forgotten than its older, more windswept counterpart.

In the short time that she had been in Ardben, Lucy had grown to love the kirk for its quaintness and rustic charm and she could picture what it might look like in the summer with the trees waving gently in the breezes and the sea showing blue through the fronds of fresh greenery. Tonight, however, she was more interested in what was going on inside the kirk, where the children of the village were gathered for a dress rehearsal. Lucy knew them all by name now, and had become very fond of them, while they in turn had grown to know and trust her, and to shyly acknowledge her whenever she met any of them in passing.

They were growing excited as their big event drew nearer and pounced on her as soon as she came through the door, all of them clamouring for attention at the same time.

Stolidly and earnestly, Miss Mary McNulty, her face flushed, her expression one of frowning solemnity, tried to retain order, but she was having great difficulty getting the 'wise men' to sing 'Away in a Manger', on cue. "You try, Lucy," she said in exasperation. "If you can exert your control over Mrs Clarrissa Campbell you can do it with a bunch of kids. I'm exhausted already and I've only just got here!"

Lucy smiled faintly at the idea of Clarrissa being compared to a bunch of kids. "Hardly the same thing, Mary, and I don't really exert any control over Clarrissa, but I'll try with the kids just the same." Clapping her hands she called for attention, then just to make sure she would get it, she took out the whistle she always carried, and on it gave three short sharp blasts.

It had an immediate effect. The children stared at her in great surprise and didn't interrupt once when she called, "Right, everybody, I want you to stand very still and listen to everything I say. When Johnny puts his gift of myrrh at the crib of the infant Jesus *that* is when you must start singing. Watch me, and listen."

Her clear young voice rang out and the children grew quiet. The little kirk was dim and mysterious with just the glow from the Christmas tree and the soft light above the manger spreading down to the nearest pews.

Lucy was engrossed in her singing. She looked little more than a child herself as she stood there, her hair a halo of pale gold against the sombre blue velvet of the pulpit cloth, her face calm and sweet as she sang the simple words of the song.

Then something stabbed into her serenity of mind, a feeling of awareness seized her and she turned to look towards the darkness at the back of the kirk. Someone

75

was there. At first she couldn't make out who it was, but her eyes soon adjusted and she saw that it was Lorn, his hands folded in front of him, his bowed head resting on top of them.

He was just a shadow, a shade darker than the other shadows that surrounded him, but she knew that it was he. She always knew when he entered any room without having to turn round or look up. His presence just seemed to reach out and touch her as if on her naked flesh.

She couldn't understand the power that this silent, unhappy man had over her but she couldn't deny that it existed. The same thing happened to her now. Just knowing that he was there in the kirk made her pulses race. Everything else seemed to fade into insignificance; no one else mattered; nothing else was important.

Her voice faltered but she sang on, though the air in her lungs felt as if it was being squeezed out of her body. As the last note echoed away he stirred and looked directly towards her. His face was a pale blur in the dimness but she knew that his eyes were burning into hers – as surely as if he was standing close beside her, gazing into her face.

Chapter Nine

He was waiting for her outside. "I went to fetch the Christmas tree," he said briefly. "I knew you would be in here and waited to see if you would like a lift home. The tree is in the trailer so there's plenty of room in the car."

A refusal sprang to her lips. She felt that to be in the car at such close proximity to him would weaken her earlier resolve. Then she realised that if she walked back she would almost certainly be late for dinner and Nora Bruce hated unpunctuality.

"Alright, Lorn," she conceded. He opened the door for her then went round to the driver's seat. The car interior was warm and comfortable and as he started up the engine she sat back, listening to the wheels scrunching over the snowy ground.

A moon was rising up over the sea, silvering the water and silhouetting the faraway hills; ripples of light whispered to the moon-bathed shore; millions of diamonds seemed to have cascaded over the landscape, winking and sparkling on the frost-rimed bracken by the roadside.

He was silent beside her and she respected his mood though she was unable to stop herself from glancing every now and then at his strong, handsome profile. The beauty of the night seeped into her, making her very aware of how precious life was and how she had grown to love Kintyre.

Then the car slowed and he pulled off the road and stopped the engine. Silence enveloped them. He kept looking straight ahead as if he wasn't seeing anything. She could smell the faint pleasing fragrance of his aftershave, mingling with the warm male scent of his body.

Abruptly he put his hand out and opening the glove compartment he extracted a small package and pushed it into her hand. "I want to give you something for all you've done for Clarrissa. I would like to have kept it for the Christmas tree but could just imagine the raised eyebrows that would draw from Nora . . ."

She opened her mouth to thank him but he put a gentle finger over her lips. "Hush, don't say anything. You mustn't open it till Christmas morning – promise."

"Yes," she said huskily. He leaned over and briefly brushed her lips with his. She could feel the heat of him, the vibration of his life forces coursing through his flesh but he drew back from her quickly, as if he was afraid of getting too close to her.

"Lucy." Her name was a mere breath in the silence. "I've missed you."

"Oh Lorn," she choked miserably. "I've missed you too. Why do you ignore my very existence?"

"Because it's the only way I can bear to live in the same house as you." His hand came up slowly and he stroked a tendril of her hair with one finger. "The moon has turned your hair from sunlight to stardust. I want to kiss it and hold you forever in my arms but – I belong to another, and your heart is in the keeping of another man."

She felt the tears bubbling out of her heart to constrict her throat and fill her eyes and when he started up the engine and the car began to move away she felt weighted to her seat with an emotion she could put no name to for it was beyond her experience.

That evening they decorated the tree in the sitting room. Lorn came through from the surgery to join them and as they hung glass baubles and threw tinsel over the sweet-smelling branches they were more unified as a family than Lucy had ever seen them.

Clarrissa was sitting in her chair, surrounded by Christmas decorations, her face sparkling with mischief as she threw tinsel over everything, including Sherry who was sitting watching proceedings with an expression of interest on his doggy face.

When Lucy had first arrived at Moorgate House, she had thought what a lovely creature Clarrissa was, but tonight, with her perfect features vibrantly alive, she was stunning. She knew it too, and shamelessly exploited the fact for her husband's benefit, but overriding her teasing remarks was a tenderness that hadn't been in her voice before.

If the phone hadn't rung that night, if the events that were about to take place could have been diverted, a happier future might have lain in store for Lorn and his wife. But it was not to be; the telephone ringing by Clarrissa's side was to change things for everyone gathered that evening in the elegant sitting room of Moorgate House.

Clarrissa lifted the receiver impatiently and put it to her ear. For a few seconds she listened, and if her face had been glowing before it now radiated pure joy. "Andrew, darling!" she cried. "How lovely to hear your voice. Where have you been? I've missed you so much!"

As Nora Bruce listened to what was being said she paused in the act of stretching up to place a star at the top of the tree and a simile of her daughter's expression transformed her dissatisfied face.

Lorn had sat down to light his pipe but when he heard his wife's exclamations on the phone his action of striking a match against the box was frozen.

Lucy felt like a spectator watching a tableau. She didn't know why a pang of dread shot through her but it did, and she sensed that everything which was in the process of mending in the house that night was very shortly about to be shattered.

Clarrissa was talking animatedly. "For Christmas? Oh you darling rogue! Meg will have a fit! The turkey isn't nearly big enough but you can have my share. . . ."

Lorn still sat completely immobile, making no effort to go and talk to the person on the other end of the phone but Nora Bruce was descending the little pair of ladders she had been using to decorate the tree and in a few strides she was by her daughter's side, her hands fluttering impatiently near the phone. When it was finally relinquished she exclaimed, "Andrew!" in much the same tone as her daughter had used when first hearing who the caller was.

Then her voice changed a little: it became harder, more brittle. "I do hope you're ashamed of yourself, Andrew. You've been neglecting us. You know how much Clarrissa enjoys you coming here and how depressed she gets when you stay away. I won't have my daughter getting upset again because when she suffers, we all suffer."

There was a short pause. Nora's face changed; whatever was being said to her over the line was obviously pleasing her and emitting an oddly girlish giggle she said indulgently, "Flatterer, you always did know how to twist us all round your little finger. *I* am not so easily swayed, however, and will expect you to be the epitomy of good behaviour while you are with us at Moorgate House."

Clarrissa wasn't listening to her mother's discourse. Her face was flushed as she spun her chair round so that she was facing Lorn. "Andrew's coming for Christmas!" She couldn't hide her pleasure and let out a little chuckle of childlike delight. "He may only be here for a few days but he's going to try for a week – a whole week! Lorn – did you hear what I said?"

"Could I help it?" His voice held the first hint of sarcasm that Lucy had ever heard him use to his wife. "Why don't you go outside and broadcast it to the entire neighbourhood? I'm sure everyone will be pleased to hear it."

He stood up and without another word made to leave the room.

"Lorn," Clarrissa's voice was cold, "fetch me my stole."

"I'll get it." Lucy got up quickly, feeling she had to escape from the scene.

"Stay where you are, Lucy. Lorn will get it, won't you dear?"

Lucy saw that his face was white with anger but wordlessly he went out to return in a short time with the stole which he placed round Clarrissa's shoulders.

She gave him no word of thanks. Instead, she said in a voice that she might use to Sherry, "Now, Lorn, get me my pills, there's a dear." Her eyes were glittering strangely.

Lucy could gladly have slapped her at that moment. She was taunting her husband, deliberately treating him like an errand boy. Any other man might have lost control of himself and Lucy felt it might be the best thing Lorn could ever do, for his wife's sake and his own. As it was he held himself back, pushed his feelings down. His jaw was tight, his fists bunching at his sides. He was bottling it all up: all the passions, the frustrations, the longings, the hurt, the anger. It was a dangerously explosive potion, like a bottle of vintage champagne with only a cork and a seal holding all the bubbles inside. Take the cork off and whoosh!

Yet, only minutes before, everything had been fine; a spirit of camaraderie had existed between everyone. Now it had all changed; the ringing of the phone, the mention of someone called 'Andrew' had brought a malignancy into what had been an unusually happy evening.

They were all back to where they had started, back to square one. Snakes and ladders, thought Lucy bitterly, only no one was winning; the snakes were too poisonous, the venom too potent to be conquered. Andrew! Who is Andrew? she wondered. She daren't ask anyone in Moorgate House that night. Lorn had gone up to bed; Clarrissa and her mother had grown silent, though there was a suppressed excitement about them.

If Lucy had known that the enigmatic Andrew was about to put an unsavoury twist into her own fate she might have packed her bags and left Moorgate House that very night. As it was she went early to bed and lay awake for a long time, thinking about many things.

On her bedside table lay the small, flat, gaily-wrapped package Lorn had given to her in the car. '*Lorn to Lucy*' was all the label said. His writing was firm but untidy and she smiled. A typical doctor's hand. Then she saw the tiny cross under her name and she touched it with a tender finger. A single kiss, so small and unobtrusive she had almost missed it, but now that she knew it was there it filled her entire vision.

His words to her in the car rang in her ears: "I've missed you, Lucy." She turned her face on the pillow to look at the moon now riding high over the Kintyre hills.

"Your hair is like stardust, tonight, Lucy." His voice echoed in her ears, the lilt of it unbearably sweet yet its persistency inside her head was oddly disturbing.

Allan's fair and handsome face floated into her mind's eye. She forced her thoughts on him. Somehow it was far safer and much less upsetting to think of Allan. She pictured him kissing her, that little smile of assurance lighting his face. . . . But it wasn't Allan's lips she felt, it was Lorn's, brushing hers briefly in the car. "Go away, Lorn," she whispered into the silent room, and a tear pricked the corner of her eyelid and rolled slowly down to her pillow.

Chapter Ten

Alone next morning in the kitchen with Meg, Lucy found out who Andrew was. Meg had just heard from Nora Bruce that he was arriving for Christmas.

"I don't like it, Lucy," Meg said slowly, her normally cheery face thoughtfully serious. "He should stay away, that he should. There's been a feeling in this house recently, as if peace were coming back to it, but that young upstart will just upset everyone again."

"Who *is* Andrew?" asked Lucy, bewildered.

"Och, you mean to say you don't know? He's Lorn's half-brother, younger than him by four years.

"Lorn's father, Alex Campbell, died when Lorn was no more than a baby, you see, and his mother re-married a couple of years later. She had Andrew soon afterwards, then her second husband died a few years after that, poor woman, and she was left to bring up the two boys on her own. God rest her, she passed away herself some years back, but she had been left comfortably off by Andrew's father, and had been able to see to it that her sons had received a good education – the best possible start in life.

"Both of them were clever laddies, but different as night and day. Andrew – his lordship, I call him! – only worked when he felt like it; fun was what he wanted most of the time, and the Lord knows he got enough of that.

As a laddie Lorn spent a lot of time standing in his wee brother's shadow. Everyone fussed over Andrew and Lorn never got a look-in.

Now, Andrew is a dashing handsome playboy if ever there was one – but likeable you understand dear; no matter what he does people can never help taking to him. And to this day, Lorn still just sinks into himself when his brother is around."

"What does he do, Andrew I mean?"

"Oh, he's a lawyer or some such thing, very fancy like, he is; every inch the city gent. But he likes coming back now and then. I don't doubt he has a soft spot for Kintyre, just as the folk here have a soft spot for him." She shook her head meaningfully and added, "Ay, some are like butter in his hands – those that haven't seen through him, that is. My Bob says he's a ladies' man, and right enough, I do believe he'd charm the pants off any lass without breaking the elastic to do so."

With that she gave Lucy a merry wink and went to put her apron on.

Andrew arrived the next day while Lucy was out Christmas shopping in Tarbert. She let herself into the hall and stood for a moment, listening to the sounds of talk and laughter coming from the sitting room, then she opened the door and paused on the threshold to take in the scene.

The room breathed of Christmas with the big tree sparkling in a corner. Beneath its tinselled boughs, gaily-wrapped parcels were heaped high; Christmas cards stood on every available space; logs crackled and hissed on the fire. Drinks had been passed round and everyone had a glass in their hand.

In a corner by the fire sat Lorn, his unlit pipe resting in an ashtray on the hearth, his long fingers restlessly playing on the stem of his glass. He was gazing into the fire, his dark eyes very far away as if he was seeing another world in the leaping flames that pranced with such abandonment up the chimney. He was there in the room with everyone else, yet he might have been in another sphere, so apart did he look from the scene.

But he knew she was there in the doorway for he looked up and straight at her, and a light, other than that from the fire, shone deep in his eyes. She smiled at him, and though they were so far apart it was as if she was beside him saying, "I'm here, please don't be lonely any more."

Clarrissa and her mother were animated, looking, as they chattered and smiled, up at the tall fair-haired man standing in the middle of the room, his back to Lucy.

Clarrissa's high, excited voice greeted Lucy affably: "Lucy, what on earth are you parked there for? Come in do, and meet Andrew Graham, Lorn's half-brother. Andrew, this is Lucy Pemberton – my nursie – Lorn thought I needed someone to hold my hand and though it hurts me to admit it, she's made a first class job of taming me these last few weeks."

Her voice went on but Lucy barely heard a word. There was a ringing in her ears, everything in the room merged and blurred. Even before the fair man turned she knew – she knew what was about to happen. It was almost as if she had waited for this moment from the time she had first set foot in Moorgate House.

The man turned slowly, and in an eternal suspension of time his deep blue eyes were upon her. How many times had she looked into those eyes before? Drowned in the charming magic of that blue, blue gaze? He was across the room in a few quick strides, his hands outstretched, his wide sensual mouth curving into that assured smile she knew so well.

The strong hands were in hers, the touch of them so well-remembered, yet the reality of them now so unbelievable she felt she must surely be dreaming. Once she had lived only for his touch; his smile; the physical strength of him holding her close to his heart; the dazzling naked yearning of his glance holding hers till she felt she would have given her soul to gaze upon him time without end.

His hands were gripping hers painfully, as if he was trying to convey to her the need for understanding, for discretion. His eyes pierced into her, pledging her into silence.

The room spun round till she thought she was going to faint and she couldn't stop the whispering sigh that escaped her white lips. "Allan . . ."

His name was a mere breath yet his eyes darkened with apprehension and he said with forced jollity, "Miss Pemberton, Lucy Pemberton, you don't mind if I call you Lucy, do you? I've been hearing so much about you I feel I know you very well already."

He was throwing her a message, begging her to refrain from letting anyone there guess that she knew him. Knew him! The others in the room might know him as Andrew Graham, but to her, he was *Allan* Graham – the man she had pined for; the man she had fled from, taking with her a heart so bruised she had thought it would never completely heal again.

But little by little it *had* been healing; bit by bit she had begun to feel happiness again – and now, here he was, bringing it all back, the hurt, the despair, the misery.

"Allan." The name was on her lips again, she couldn't help it, she had to convince herself that she wasn't dreaming, that here in front of her was the man she had tried to escape from all those long weeks ago.

"Andrew!" Clarrissa's voice came sharply at this point, imperative, querulous. "What on earth is going on? Do you two know one another? Is this some sort of conspiracy? If so, I want to know all about it, and the sooner the better for all of us."

Nora Bruce was nodding her agreement, all the while looking at Lucy in a most suspicious manner. Lorn too was gazing curiously at both Lucy and his brother, a strange, dark expression flitting over his face as he waited for either one of them to speak.

The pupils of the fair man's eyes had dilated, and with a clumsy movement he stepped back a pace and stumbled against an occasional table. The glass he was holding slipped from his hands and shattered on the table top, some of the pieces scattering over the carpet. He stooped quickly to pick them up while Nora Bruce rushed for the brush and shovel on the hearth.

"Hell, I've cut myself!" His half-laughing little yelp of pain sounded genuine and he straightened, sucking at his finger. "Lucy, you're a nurse – could you do something for an injured soldier?"

"Don't stand back!" yelped Nora Bruce. "You'll crush the glass into the carpet!" She fussed with the brush, seemingly more concerned with the mess than she was with the cut finger though she did look up and say, "Go on then, Miss Pemberton, can't you see the boy needs attention?"

"A timely intervention." Clarrissa's voice came sarcastically, her eyes boring into Lucy as she spoke. "Are you sure you didn't arrange it to suit yourself, Andrew?"

He didn't reply. Instead, he took Lucy's arm to hastily propel her out of the room, across the hall and into the kitchen where he began to speak to her rapidly. "Lucy, darling, for God's sake pretend you've just met me. It would cause a war back there if it were discovered we already know one other. God! How they would go on, and I just couldn't take it at the present time. I'd an idea you would be here, that's why I came. My sweet darling, I've been out of my mind since you left – look, get me something for this hand in case anyone comes through – I'll explain everything if you'll just listen."

In a daze she went to the cupboard where a first aid box held bandages and sticking plaster. *I don't understand, I don't understand.* The protests rang in her head, even as she knew the answers. Allan had often spoken to her about his home in Kintyre, a softness in his voice when he had described to her the endless sea; the lush farmlands; the moors; the hills.

In the warm circle of his arms she had listened to him talking of his boyhood days; days of swimming, fishing, walking in the sweet lands of his childhood. In her fleeing from him she had subconsciously sought the place where his feet had trod, his voice had rung, and in so doing a strange quirk of fate had carried her to the very house in which he had grown up.

He was talking again, his voice rushing like a hill burn through the troubled valleys of her mind. "Your parents wouldn't tell me where you were but that old lady of yours, the one you looked after in London, she was very helpful. She remembered me you see, recalled

89

my calling for you one night, and she said she thought then how much in love we were. She let it slip you were in Kintyre so I came to look for you – never dreaming for one moment to find you in this very house I consider my country home. . . ."

Nora Bruce came through at that moment to empty the broken glass into the waste bin and she threw him a rather meaningful look. "Don't be long *Andrew* dear, we must make full use of every minute you are here. Clarrissa has been so looking forward to your coming. You've stayed away from her for far too long and the two of you have a lot of catching up to do."

She turned to Lucy and her eyes were glittering slightly when she said, "You won't keep him, will you, Miss Pemberton?"

Lucy shook her head wordlessly and turned away, a thousand questions trembling on her lips.

But Allan – *Andrew* – gave her no chance to speak. As soon as Nora left the room he turned to Lucy and, spreading his hands, he said beseechingly, "Darling, please look at me and say you've forgiven me – I made a mistake but it's all over and I promise you it won't happen again – surely we're all allowed one mistake in our lives! I know I hurt you and I'm sorry. You're my only love. I jeopardised everything we had in a moment of weakness, and after you had gone from me I knew it was only you I ever wanted. Forgive me my sweet, darling, innocent little Lucy."

Her legs were like jelly beneath her and she sat down to look at him in disbelief. "So – you're Andrew – *Andrew* Graham – not *Allan* Graham; your very name was a lie to me."

He looked downcast. "Oh, don't make it sound like such a bad crime, Lucy, lots of people call themselves

90

by different names, and my full title is Andrew Allan Graham, so I wasn't really cheating anyone. I was never all that keen on Andrew – patriotic and all that, but I felt like a change, and on impulse, I called myself by my middle name when I met you. Perhaps it was silly of me, I see that now. I just thought Allan suited me better – somehow it had a ring to it."

"I see," she said woodenly.

"Lucy." He was beside her, his hands on her shoulders, his eyes searching her face, then his lips were on hers, soft, warm, irresistibly gentle, so unlike the sensual demanding mouth she remembered so well.

He was like a little boy begging forgiveness. The fragile shell she had built protectively round her heart cracked easily to allow him in once more. His lips caressed her hair, her face, then came to her mouth again. This time it was hard with passion, his tongue probing till it found hers, and she began to respond against her will.

Somewhere deep in her bewildered mind she compared him to Lorn. Night and day, Meg had said they were. How right she was. Lorn was so different. She had rejected him and he had moved away from her, too proud, too respectful, too used to the loneliness of his life to push himself forward, even if it meant unhappiness for the rest of his days.

Allan/Andrew refused to be pushed aside. If he wanted something or someone he went all out till he got his way. He was sophisticated, witty, charming, in control of himself and all that he claimed; so suave, it was difficult to believe he was of Highland stock.

His very voice held no trace of his Scottish upbringing. Lorn's voice was sweetly cultured, as musical as the burns that flowed from the wild Scottish hills. Andrew's voice

91

held no trace of accent – except – she remembered now – when he was off-guard, had drunk a little too much, an inflection had crept in, an inheritance of the Highlands.

He was kissing her deeper, his lips playing with hers, the desires of his body burning into her in fiery waves. A little moan rose deep in his throat, his body was as taut as a bowstring, he was forgetting where he was, forgetting all, in his physical yearnings.

His fingers were digging into her arms, she could feel his male hardness against her. This quick arousal of his had always touched a chord of unease in her . . . yet she couldn't resist the warmth of him, the burning heat that pulsated through him to her . . . until . . .

"Andrew, Andrew! Where *are* you?" Clarrissa's voice came querulously and the high whine of her chair sounded in the hall.

Lucy pushed Andrew away.

Beads of perspiration were standing out on his forehead and his blue eyes were misty with longing. "Damn her," he swore crossly. "Look, let me come to your room tonight, honey."

She had no time to voice her refusal. Clarrissa was in the kitchen regarding them quizzically. Andrew had hastily resumed his position in a chair opposite Lucy who, with shaking fingers, was blindly wrapping a piece of elastoplast round his proffered finger.

"You two have been in here a long time." Clarrissa's eyes were dark with suspicion.

"I couldn't find the first aid box," lied Lucy. "There, that should do the trick. It's not a very deep cut." Her voice was low with the effort of trying to speak normally. "I must go now and get off these outdoor things."

"You're all flushed-looking," Clarrissa persisted, gazing

92

enquiringly from one to the other. "Both of you. Just what have you been up to, I wonder?"

Lucy took a deep shuddering breath. "It's no use, I can't pretend, not even for you, Allan, or should *I* call you Andrew too, now? You're right, Clarrissa, we did know one another, it was all a long time ago and it's over now, so please, don't take it so much to heart."

She was aware of Andrew's furiously reproachful glance, Clarrissa's intake of breath, her burning eyes, her momentary shocked silence, before she spoke again.

"Really, Andrew," she said, in a curiously flat voice, "I thought you knew better than to try and fool me. At least Lucy has had the decency to tell me the truth, and even though I'm not at all pleased with her I appreciate her for her honesty."

Glancing witheringly from one to the other she went on in a tone she might have used to a pair of naughty schoolchildren. "You really have been an awfully long time in here. I will give you the benefit of the doubt and assume that you have just been sorting everything out between you."

She moved restlessly in her chair and said peevishly, "Come along now, Andrew, you came here to visit *me*, remember? And we have a great deal of catching up to do. Mother has poured the drinks and everything is nice and cosy for us in the sitting room."

With a rather sheepish glance at Lucy, Andrew followed Clarrissa from the room, and Lucy was left, staring into space, her mind going round in circles as she tried to sort out everything that had happened since she came in from her shopping trip.

The evening that followed was rather strained. Lorn hardly spoke a word; Nora Bruce was equally restrained;

Clarrissa was broody and snappish. Only Andrew seemed unaffected by everything, and chattered away breezily about every subject under the sun.

Then Clarrissa spilt her drink all over her expensive oyster satin blouse, and when her mother and Lorn rushed forward to help she pushed them away and began to weep uncontrollably.

"Oh, come on now, Rissa," Andrew said to her in jocular tones, "it isn't the end of the world. Surely you must have something else to change into; your wardrobes are stuffed with clothes."

"It isn't that!" Clarrissa stormed at him. "It's just . . . everything seems to have gone wrong tonight and I had planned it all so differently."

She fell once more to a storm of weeping, but no one was in the mood to put up with her tantrums when all their nerves were raw and ready to snap at the least provocation.

Clarrissa ranted and raved, she wept and sobbed, she wouldn't listen to reason of any sort, and in the end Lorn had to put her to bed and give her a sedative, and it was a very subdued household who later went about their separate affairs, none of them daring to look at one another or say very much in case it might cause further upsets.

Chapter Eleven

That night, Lucy locked her bedroom door, something she had never dreamed of doing when it was just herself and Lorn sharing the upper landing. She wouldn't give in to Andrew as easily as he obviously imagined she would. She had to have time to collect her scattered wits. She felt cheated of everything she had tried to regain in the way of pride and dignity yet the thought of Allan – or Andrew – she had to think of him now as Andrew – just a few paces away – quickened her heart.

Lorn crept into her thoughts, Lorn alone, apart from everyone, and even more remote and withdrawn since the arrival of his brother who seemed not to notice or care.

She wondered why she felt so miserable. She should have been brimming over with anticipation. The man she loved, the man she had unconsciously set out to find, was here, inside the sturdy walls of Moorgate House.

With a little start she was aware that the handle of her door was slowly turning. Her heart bounded faster.

"Lucy, are you awake? Let me in." Andrew's whisper came eerily through the darkness.

She lay quite still and silent, every muscle in her body tensed. "Lucy, darling, I know you're awake, please let me speak to you."

She made no sound. A minute passed; a minute filled

with the sound of her own heart beating in her ears and the tangible feel of Andrew waiting outside her door.

Then came a muffled word she couldn't catch but knew that it was an oath of disgust. Soft footsteps padded away and every shrieking nerve in her body quietened and slowly she relaxed. Tomorrow she would be better able to cope with the situation but tonight she was too bewildered, too weary to cope with herself, let alone Andrew.

She tossed and turned all night and awoke feeling as if a weight was dragging her down to the bottom of a troubled sea. She swung her legs over the edge of the bed and sat shivering as the cold air of morning swept over her.

The first thing that caught her eye was Lorn's parcel on the table. Lifting it she looked again at the Christmassy label. *Lorn to Lucy.* Somehow it had a ring to it. She was Lucy to him now, even if he went on calling her 'Miss Pemberton' in front of others. In his heart he thought of her as Lucy.

Somewhere inside herself a little nerve of joy began to quiver. It was Christmas Eve. She had always loved Christmas but this one was going to be special, different. Clarrissa had told her she could go home for Christmas but she had opted to wait for the New Year. It was a personal tradition of hers always to bring in the bells with her parents in the house where she was born.

Throwing on her dressing-gown she padded over to the window. It was a soft blue morning, calm and hazy with the snow-capped hills slumbering serenely against the gold-streaked sky. The sea was tinged with turquoise, a gentle sea sparkling in this the Eve of Christ's birth.

"Away in a manger . . ." The children's voices seemed to be carried to her on the tranquil breath of morning, and she could imagine a heavenly choir of them, sitting on that

little puffball cloud above the cliffs, their faces shining in cherubic innocence.

She had to smile at this flagrant vision. Often they were more like little devils than angels, yet a smile from them, a heart-warming gesture, a simple small gift, could transform them into the dearest little souls she had ever encountered.

She loved them all. They weren't precocious children and she had become entranced with their natural charm and the unaffected joy they extracted from their lives.

She smiled again. Johnny had tripped on his way to the crib during the last rehearsal. Tonight was the night and she hoped it would all go well, yet somehow she knew that it was all the little mistakes, the unconscious humour, the unexpected gestures, that made the things that children did a joy to behold.

Even if Johnny fell at the foot of the crib it would in no way detract from the pleasure of the onlooker. Humming a carol she gathered up her toilet things and made her way to the bathroom.

She emerged, fresh and tingling after her shower and bumped into Andrew coming from his room. He was rumpled and handsome, his fair head shining, his eyes bluer than the sea she had recently gazed upon.

Without hesitation he caught her and kissed her. "You smell of toothpaste," he laughed, his own teeth very white in a face that was bronzed, even in winter. "You locked your door last night," he accused, a spark of irritation in his eyes. "Don't you want me, Lucy? Have you forgotten everything we had together?"

She was annoyed to feel her heart beginning to accelerate. "Of course not – it's just . . ."

"Darling little Lucy – afraid of the big bad wolf." He

pulled her closer and cupped her face in his hands to look at her. "Lucy, Lucy, it's Christmas. If I promise to be a good boy will you be a Christmas angel and grant me a wish?"

"Stop that!" she told him angrily. "I'm not here to grant you anything, and how can you behave like this when Clarrissa so obviously adores you and acts as if she has some sort of claim on you?"

"Oh c'mon, baby, you know Clarrissa, she must have little dramas in her life. I just happen to be the one she's picked on to keep her amused for the moment. We're just friends, that's all; she would like to make it into something bigger but I'm not going to get caught that easily."

As he was speaking his fingers were creeping into the damp curls at the nape of Lucy's neck, forcing her face closer to his, playfully seeking her lips.

"No, no, stop it, leave me alone!" she said angrily, planting her clenched fists against his broad chest in an effort to break free of his grasp. But the more she struggled the tighter he held on, his teeth flashing with amusement.

"Playing hard to get, eh? You shouldn't do that, Lucy, you know how exciting I find it." Roughly he pulled her in closer and his lips came down hard on hers. She tried to cry out but she was smothering – not with excitement because he was kissing her – but with apprehension in case Lorn should come out of his room and see them.

Even as she struggled she wondered at herself. These were the lips she loved – had longed for – but she felt none of the old emotions rising within her.

"Darling," he murmured urgently in her ear, "come into my room – only for a little while – I just want – to love you . . ."

A little click came from somewhere nearby and without looking up she knew it was Lorn. With burning cheeks she pulled herself out of Andrew's grasp and her eyes, huge with embarrassment, looked to where Lorn was standing outside his room. His face was white, an expression of contempt twisted his fine features, and she knew what he was thinking, how the situation must look to him, that she was allowing herself to be kissed by a man, who to all accounts, had been a perfect stranger to her until yesterday.

She wanted to cry out, "I know him, this is Allan, the man I left England to escape." Instead she lowered her eyes, unable to face the disbelief in his.

He brushed past them without a word and Andrew gave a chuckle of amusement. "Oh, c'mon, big brother," he teased, "don't look so shocked, and don't turn round and tell me honestly that you wouldn't give a lot to do what I've just been doing. Anyway, we aren't doing anything so wrong. Lucy and I knew one another intimately in England, so there's no need for you to get so worked up about us merely kissing. You know the score now, I'm being honest with you, so there's no need for you to look like that."

Lorn halted. With a stony expression he came back to face his brother, his jaw tense, his fingers bunching into fists at his sides. "If honesty was a policy of this house you would have been told what you were long ago and booted out of it while you were still in short trousers," he snapped.

His gaze swept over Lucy, cool and disdainful, before he turned about and went downstairs.

She faced Andrew, her own face white with anger. "That was despicable, talking as if you and I were still seeing one another when you know it's all over between us. And how dare you speak about me as if I was something for you to play with whenever the mood takes you. I came here to get away from you – Allan – Andrew – whatever you care to call yourself – and I will thank you to keep your hands off me and to stop pestering me in my room at night. My door is locked to you and will remain so till *I* feel like letting you in."

She had never spoken to him in such a manner, had never imagined she could, and a flush of anger darkened his face. But then he was smiling again with assurance, and telling her, "You love me, Lucy, and I won't let you forget it, make no mistake about that."

And he kept to his word. Whenever they were alone together, or when he passed her, he would lay his hand intimately on her arm and squeeze it, and several times his lips brushed hers.

She was annoyed at these liberties. "What right has he got?" she asked herself. "He doesn't own me." Yet even while her mind protested, her heart flipped over at the feel of his lips on hers, and she wondered, as she had wondered so often before, if she would ever be strong enough to really break free of the spell that Andrew Graham had over her.

That afternoon, he took Clarrissa and her mother for a drive in a car as streamlined as himself. He had pressed Lucy to come too but she made some excuse and stood at the window, watching the sleek, peach-coloured Mercedes purring down the driveway, then she wandered round the sitting room feeling deserted and terribly sad, though she didn't know quite why.

100

The pile of parcels under the tree caught her eye, and with a start she realised she had bought a small gift for everyone except Lorn. And Andrew too of course – she hadn't expected to see him this Christmas.

Yet *had* she forgotten to buy something for Lorn? Or had her mind deliberately shut him out, because a small reminder for him simply wouldn't do. It had to be something special, yet it couldn't be. Special things were for special people and he was, after all, just her employer. Besides, she couldn't have the others talking, saying she favoured him above everyone else.

It had to be all – or nothing – yet, even as her mind raced, she was pulling on her outdoor clothes and letting herself out of the house.

There were few shops in Ardben but without hesitation she made her way to the fishing tackle store and was soon describing what she wanted to the toothless, white-bearded ancient who presided there.

Clarissa had mentioned that Lorn was fond of sea-fishing and the old man knew exactly what sort of rod it was that she rather hazily described.

"If I go and get some gift paper from the grocer would you wrap it up, Angus?" she asked, smilingly. "I've never wrapped up a fishing rod before."

"You get the paper, lass, and I'll bind it up for you," grinned Angus gummily. "Must do the job right for a fine rod like this – best one I've got in the store – must be for someone special – eh?"

"Not really, it's just . . . I didn't know what else would be suitable," faltered Lucy, and she went quickly out of the shop and over to the grocer who sold everything from butter to boot polish.

While she was there a display of gifts caught her eye

and she hastily chose a tiepin for Andrew which, though not up to his expensive tastes, would just have to do, she decided firmly.

Briefly, she wondered at herself. Last Christmas she had trod the streets of London till she was footsore and weary, searching out an elaborate and expensive gift for him. Even after she had purchased it she had brooded over it, wondering if it was good enough for him, hoping that it would please him.

She had been very anxious to please in those days; too anxious. Perhaps that had been part of the trouble. She had spoiled him; but he had demanded that sort of attention. Now she knew why. According to Meg people had always spoiled Andrew, and she believed implicitly that Meg was not the sort of person to exaggerate.

She trudged homewards, lifting her face to the skies which were piled thickly now, with grey lowering clouds hanging threateningly over the horizon. The gulls wheeled noisily over the cliffs, as if protesting at the change in the weather. Ragged purple-grey clouds were rolling over the hill peaks, spilling snow flurries into the corries. The salt air stung her cheeks and she breathed deeply and murmured, "I love you, Kintyre of the sea and the hills. I love you even in your nastier moods."

She was wind-tossed and sparkling when she arrived back. The house was warm and silent. No one was back yet. It was too early for Meg, who went home after lunch each day and came back later in the afternoon. Lorn had been out most of the day on calls and wouldn't possibly be back till near evening surgery.

There was no respite for him, not even on Christmas Eve but Dr Millar had promised to be on call for the next two days, so at least the younger doctor would be able to relax over Christmas.

Humming a little tune she went to put the kettle on to make herself some tea and found Lorn in the kitchen, a mug of tea at his elbow, his pipe in his mouth. She sensed him stiffening at the sight of her, and in confusion she said, "Lorn, I'm so glad you're in, I've got something for you and I want you to have it now. The others will be opening their things tomorrow and I didn't want you to think I had forgotten you – I'll – get it."

She went to the hall where she had propped the awkwardly-shaped parcel, and feeling slightly ridiculous she carried it into the kitchen. "I don't really know the sort of things you like but Clarissa mentioned . . . well, I'll let you open it – I hope it's alright. Angus said . . ."

He stood up, his eyes glittering with ill-concealed annoyance. He made no move to take the package from her. "Miss Pemberton, there is no call for you to go spending your money on me." His voice was so icily cold she shivered. "You are here in this house for one reason and one reason only – to look after my wife and to make her as happy as possible in the circumstances. . . . Now, if you will excuse me, I have things to do."

She recoiled from him but could not refrain from crying out, "If you are angry because of – of what you saw and heard this morning then you are wrong, Lorn, oh – please . . ."

"What you do in your own time is no concern of mine, Miss Pemberton," he told her harshly. "Do not feel for one moment that you have to explain away your actions to me."

She stood there, the fishing rod in her hand, feeling foolish and angry. "Go on then, go your own solitary

103

way, Lorn Campbell!" she cried in a voice choked with tears. "I can see now you enjoy being a martyr. You're selfish and spoiled – you and Clarrissa make a fine pair – oh, and not forgetting that brother of yours – you all need a good sound spanking to bring you to your senses!"

With a lump in her throat she flew past him, and up the stairs to her room where she wrenched open the cupboard door and threw the package containing the fishing rod right to the back, then she collapsed on the bed and fell to a storm of weeping.

All the pent up emotions of the past few weeks erupted and burst out of her. She would leave this house! She would pack her bags and go this very night! She couldn't stand any of it – any of them a minute longer. For several minutes she wept and raged then slowly she sat up and fumbling for a hanky she blew her nose hard.

No! She would *not* leave! She laughed mirthlessly. She couldn't, even if she wanted to, unless she walked. She wasn't in London now, with buses running every few minutes.

Why should she leave anyway? She wouldn't be driven away. How Nora Bruce would love that, how Andrew would smile with triumph and think she was going back to the city – to be with him.

Doors slammed below. There was the sound of voices and loud laughter. Clarrissa was home. She would be wanting to freshen up and get dressed for dinner – extra-specially dressed: tonight was Christmas Eve, Andrew was here, last night had been gloomy and dreadful, but now everyone was being very merry and exuberant – except of course, for Lorn who was seldom anything else but unhappy now.

She got up and went to the window to look out. The

clouds were showering snow over the countryside. It was drifting down like confetti. It was a white Christmas, a dazzling, perfect white Christmas.

She straightened, and her mouth curved into a smile. Tonight she would not have to sit at the dinner table listening to senseless small talk and watch Clarrissa fawning over Andrew. Nora too seemed to have forgiven him for his neglect of her daughter and she would also be fawning and fussing and laughing at all the little amusing things he had to say.

But Lucy wouldn't be there to see any of it. The Sunday school Nativity was starting at eight-thirty and all those dear little cherubs with their fresh eager young faces would be there under the soft lights, entrancing all the folk attending the early Christmas Eve service in Ardben kirk.

She hoped when Johnny laid his gift of myrrh at the crib the others would remember it was their cue to start singing. . . .

The clouds were parting, a star big and bright shone in the heavens, the moon was riding behind a silver-lined cloud. "*Silent night, Holy night . . .*" she crooned softly, and thought, "It *is* going to be calm and bright after all."

It was an omen. Life was full of storms which made the calm all the more precious.

Chapter Twelve

On Christmas morning she awoke feeling very peaceful and lay for a luxurious ten minutes thinking about the service the night before. It had gone perfectly, with the children singing like little angels, their faces shining with joy.

The congregation had been captivated, and in the absolute peace of the tiny kirk it really seemed as if the spirit of the Divine Love was there in the midst of the people, touching them with the joy of the occasion.

Lucy had been in many churches in her life, but never had she felt so moved as in that small intimate place of worship. And later, outside, everyone wished her the season's greetings, their soft Highland voices melting into the frosty air, the kirk looking like something from an old-fashioned Christmas card sitting amidst the sparkling tracts of snow, the light from the open door spilling a golden pathway onto the white land outside, cascading warmly over those who lingered to shake the minister's hand.

Her thoughts made her sigh with contentment and she turned her head slowly on the pillow to see Lorn's parcel lying beside her alarm clock. For the last three mornings it was the first thing she had glimpsed on waking and it had given her an odd feeling of warmth to remember how he had handed it to her in the car, and his tender words when she had questioned his distant attitude towards her: "It's the only way I can bear to live in the same house as you. I want to hold you forever in my arms. . . ."

Now he seemed to loathe the very sight of her, and after the scene with him yesterday he had grown further away from her than ever.

She sat up and fingered the parcel. "I won't open it," she told herself angrily. "He wouldn't open mine to him."

He had told her he didn't want *anything* from her and that, more than anything, was the thing that hurt.

For quite some time her fingers moved over the gay wrapping paper, then in a burst of rage she snatched the parcel up. "I'll show him I'm not the moody child he is," she thought fiercely, and with trembling hands she tore off the paper and opened the small oblong box. It was a necklace; a tiny silver heart on a silver chain, nestling in a bed of red satin.

Picking it up she let it dangle from her fingers. It was exquisite; small but expensive, and she lay back on her pillows to stare at it lying in her hand. "I will wear you this very morning," she whispered. "It is Christmas and Lorn Campbell has given me a silver heart to wear at my throat."

She arose and went to her wardrobe. She would wear something special today, she thought, and took out a pale blue V-necked angora dress. Quickly she slipped it on then she brushed her corn-coloured curls till they shone – and lastly she took the necklace from its box and clasped it round her neck. It nestled against her skin, unobtrusive yet eye-catching. He would see it and realise what a baby he had been yesterday.

She examined her face in the mirror. Normally she

never had time for make-up but this was a special day. Everyone else would no doubt make a bigger effort than usual, and hurriedly she applied a touch of lipstick and a smudge of slate blue eyeshadow. It would have to do; she had spent too much time looking at Lorn's little silver heart. Clarrissa would be waiting for her and she was a young woman who didn't like to be kept waiting by anybody.

Normally Clarrissa had breakfast in bed, but was getting up for it this morning. Andrew was the reason, of course. Clarrissa had obviously developed quite a fierce attachment to him and was possessive and jealous if he dared to spend more than a few minutes out of her company.

Lucy knew that she had still to face an interrogation on the subject of her past relations with him. Clarrissa hadn't yet had an opportunity to really enlarge on the subject but it would come, Lucy was quite certain of that, and when she eventually made her way downstairs to Clarrissa's room she had to compose herself for a few moments outside the door before she turned the handle and went in.

As expected, Clarrissa was sitting up in bed, positively glaring in the direction of the door, her impatience showing in the spark of disapproval in her eyes and the restless tapping of her long fingers on the tea tray that her mother had brought to her earlier.

"Where *have* you been?" she demanded irritably. "I've been waiting ages! I hope you're not going to become a lie-a-bed, Lucy Pemberton! The last one tried that and was soon sent packing."

"The 'last one' probably collapsed with exhaustion and was perhaps glad to get 'sent packing' as you put it," Lucy replied with a tilt of her firm little chin. "You aren't exactly a serene spirit to deal with, Clarrissa."

108

"Careful, Lucy," the older girl returned warningly. "You can't just say what you like to me, you know, and if I had been a really spiteful sort of person I *would* have sent you packing after finding out what I did about you and Andrew."

Lucy said nothing, but firmly stood her ground, and there was a glint of admiration in Clarrissa's eyes as she held Lucy's gaze. In the end it was she who was the first to turn her eyes away since it was evident that Lucy wasn't going to be browbeaten into humility on any account.

"As a matter of fact," Clarrissa drawled, making a great play of folding the napkin lying on her tray, "I do very much want to know what went on between you and Andrew. Were you in love with him, Lucy Pemberton?"

"I thought I was," Lucy said woodenly, keeping her eyes averted as she spoke. "I told you, it's over now."

"Is it? Are you quite sure of that?" Clarrissa probed with annoying persistency. "When you first came to us you were quite an unhappy wee thing. It was obvious you were hankering after something or someone. Now I know it was Andrew you were weeping for and I think I have a right to ask these questions."

"Ask all you like," Lucy said quietly. "But everyone has a right to privacy in their lives and all you need to know is that you don't have to worry about Andrew and me any more. I have no claim on him, he has none on me. He's a free agent as far as I'm concerned and you're welcome to him."

"But, how long did you know one another?" Clarrissa cried, tears of frustration dancing in her eyes. "Where did you meet? *When* did you meet? Did you love him? Did he love you? Lucy Pemberton, I *demand* that you tell me all about it. I have a right to be told. Because of you he

109

neglected me and I was so miserable I wanted to curl up and die."

"You're married to Lorn, Clarrissa, how can you speak like that about Andrew when you have a man like Lorn for your husband?"

Clarrissa laughed mirthlessly. "Oh, come on now, Lucy, don't act the little goody with me. My liking Andrew doesn't matter to Lorn, he knows that his brother and me are kindred spirits and that if Andrew keeps me amused then everybody is happy. I'm a bitch when I'm unhappy, Lucy, everybody suffers, but when I'm feeling good I spread it around and it rubs off on everyone who touches me."

"Your husband doesn't seem very pleased about Andrew being here."

"Oh, Lorn! Nothing pleases him these days . . ." she slid Lucy a sidelong glance, "except, perhaps, you, Nurse Lucy Pemberton."

Lucy was caught off guard and blushed to the roots of her hair. "Stop it, Clarrissa, you go too far. Your husband adores you and no one else, and stop worrying about Andrew, I've no doubt you can twist him around your little finger as you do everyone else. One snap and he comes running."

At that, Clarrissa clapped her hands together gleefully and throwing back her dark head she let out a peal of delighted laughter which made Lucy smile too. When the older woman laughed it was infectious and allowed a glimpse to another side of her nature that was charming and attractive.

Clarrissa then ordered that a selection of garments be brought for her to choose from. She couldn't make up her mind and Lucy began to feel exasperated. Clarrissa had too many clothes, that was her trouble, yet Lucy had to admit, whatever she wore she wore beautifully. Her taste was impeccable; she knew unerringly what sort of outfit each occasion demanded.

She finally decided on a rose pink, pure silk trouser suit which privately Lucy thought was far too glamorous to wear at breakfast, even though it was Christmas.

She was flushed and over-excited, grabbing the hairbrush from Lucy to pull it irritably through her thick dark tresses before she charged away in her chair, leaving Lucy to gather up all the discarded clothes and place them on their hangers in the wardrobe.

Breakfast was not being served in the kitchen as usual. Clarrissa had insisted they all eat in the dining room and Lucy made her way there, realising she would be the last to be seated.

"Come along, Miss Pemberton," shrilled Nora Bruce. "Don't you know we're all waiting for you?"

All eyes focused on Lucy and she felt the blood flooding her face. Andrew was smiling, open admiration in eyes that appraised her from head to foot. Lorn glanced up at her briefly before turning away but it was enough for her to know he had noticed the necklace: he had given himself away by looking straight at it before lowering his eyes.

Clarrissa was quick to notice Andrew's appreciative gaze fixed on Lucy as she took her place at the table and anger darkened her face. "Nursie," she drawled in sarcastic acknowledgement, "how sweet you look this morning. I wore a lot of baby blue when I was a little girl."

"And now, Rissa, you wear baby pink," laughed Andrew teasingly.

"I wear what suits me, darling, some people have a knack for it . . . others . . ." She let her words hang

111

mockingly in midair and Lucy, sitting between her and Andrew, went redder still.

"Meeow," said Andrew, his eyes still on Lucy. "You shouldn't be such a little cat, Rissa, in my opinion Lucy looks charming this happy Christmas morn . . ."

"And in mine she's the freshest most natural girl I've seen for a long time." It was Lorn's voice, cutting through Andrew's, quietly and gently, yet bringing more attention on himself than any of the others with their too-loud comments.

"Well, big brother, you are full of little surprises," said Andrew in amusement, his smile curving his lips but not reaching his eyes. "I hope your sudden appreciation for the female sex extends itself to your wife."

Clarrissa too was smiling but it was an artificial smile. Jealousy flashed out of her eyes. "Oh, I could dress in sack cloth and Lorn would never notice," she said bitterly.

Lorn's eyes glinted angrily. "That is not true, Clarrissa, and damned fine you know it! I'm always telling you how beautiful you look but I will not sit here and listen to you demeaning Miss Pemberton after all she's done for you – for us all."

Lucy placed her napkin on the table and stood up, feeling that she couldn't bear another moment in that room. The air was heavy with a resentment that was stifling. "I think I'll go out for a walk – I – I don't feel very hungry."

"Oh, sit down, Lucy." Clarrissa for once looked ashamed of herself. "I am a catty bitch, you should be used to me by now – and you mustn't worry about me and Lorn arguing, we do it quite often, surely you must have heard us at it. It's strange: they say that opposites get on well together

112

yet you could never meet a more opposite pair than Lorn and me and we seem to do nothing but get on each other's nerves."

Lucy sank slowly into her seat once more just as Nora Bruce came through with the orange juice. She had surpassed herself that morning. The table was beautifully set. A bowl of Christmas roses stood to one side and there was a centrepiece of perfumed candles floating in water, surrounded by holly, ivy and button dahlias. A hostess trolley near the table contained bacon, kidneys, fish, sausages and eggs. It was a feast which Lucy had looked forward to but the smell of which now nauseated her, having quickly lost her appetite soon after making her appearance in the dining room.

Nora Bruce's dark eyes came to rest on Lucy who was amazed to see a glint of sympathy lurking in their depths. She had of course heard every word from the kitchen and as she put a glass at Lucy's place she seemed to be searching for something appeasing to say and finally came out with a complimentary remark. "What a lovely and charming necklace, Miss Pemberton. From someone special, no doubt?"

Lucy's head came up and she said clearly and firmly, "Yes, Mrs Bruce, from someone very special."

"Oh, do tell us," gushed Clarrissa, "I love a romance."

"For heaven's sake, Rissa!" Andrew's face was creased with annoyance and Lucy thought that he didn't look nearly so handsome when he wasn't wearing a smile.

Nora Bruce sat down and said thoughtfully, "I couldn't help hearing what you were all talking about just now and you know . . ." she put one elbow on the table and propped up her chin with her thumb, "it set me thinking – about opposites. As Clarrissa said, she and Lorn are complete

113

opposites – yet – do they get on? Well, I for one have still to see it."

An eerie silence had descended over the room but she went on determinedly, "Miss Pemberton and Andrew now, both as fair as cornfields but that of course is only skin deep, they have entirely different natures. Andrew is . . ." Here she stopped to regard him quizzically. "Andrew is a charmer, always full of fun, everybody wants to be where he is and he loves to be surrounded by people. Miss Pemberton on the other hand . . ." Her eyes looked straight into Lucy's and they were no longer sympathetic; calculating was the word for the expression in them as she went on: "Miss Pemberton is a reserved, simple sort of girl, she doesn't at all like the limelight, do you, dear? No, she gets upset easily, also she takes life somewhat seriously. She and Andrew are complete opposites. Sexual attraction might lead them to at first think they were a good match for one another but it wouldn't work."

Lucy reddened again and wondered wildly just how much the older woman knew. Andrew had hardly been discreet during his encounters with her and it was just possible that Nora Bruce had spied them embracing and didn't like the idea of it one bit. She would know by now, of course, that they weren't strangers to each other, Clarrissa must have said something, and it looked as if her mother was hell bent on making certain that nothing else happened that might possibly keep Andrew and her daughter apart.

"Hey, c'mon." Andrew was looking slightly annoyed. "That's taking things a bit far. And where is all this leading anyway? How do you know I wouldn't get on with Lucy?"

"Pure assumption, my dear Andrew," rebuked Nora

Bruce. "And do let me finish, I'm having fun. I was coming to you and Clarrissa – my beautiful raven-haired Clarrissa: her colouring is so different from yours yet you both have the same personalities – vibrant, fun-loving, outgoing, the centre of all eyes – you are not opposites, yet you make a perfect match for each other."

There was complete silence now. Andrew and Clarrissa looked acutely embarrassed and Lucy simply couldn't bring herself to observe Lorn's reactions. She had known from the start that Nora Bruce was a ruthless woman, one who conveyed quite plainly without words, her disapproval of her daughter's choice of marriage partner, but to sit here, on Christmas morning, and openly voice such inflammatory opinions, was almost beyond belief.

Her high voice was going on, "Miss Pemberton and Lorn now, they are so alike in many ways . . ."

Lorn's fist crashed down on the table with such force that a fork fell to the floor. "That is *enough!*" he raged in a fury so intense that Lucy thought, "This is it, the bubbles are about to burst."

His face was so white she thought he was going to strike out at his mother-in-law but after the preliminary outburst his voice and manner became menacingly calm. "I will have no more of this foolish talk in *my* house. This is Christmas morning. Can we – just for once in our lives – behave like a normal family with the intention only of enjoying this day? For God's sake, *can* we?" He was breathing heavily, his rage-darkened eyes glaring at Nora Bruce, who, with maddening calm, was raising her glass of juice to her lips as if nothing had happened and that Lorn's outburst was of little importance to her.

Clarrissa too was white and tense looking and she was beginning to tremble. "For pity's sake, Mother, Lorn's

115

right, you can be a damned old hellcat when you put your mind to it. . . . Oh – I feel sick – Lorn – can you get me something?"

He threw down his napkin. "Now see what you've done," he gritted at his mother-in-law, before striding quickly from the room, banging the door behind him.

Chapter Thirteen

As soon as he had left, Nora Bruce put down her glass and glancing from Clarrissa to Andrew she said laughingly, "Oh, c'mon you two, you know I'm right: you were made for each other, right from the moment you met. Pity it had to be after Clarrissa was well and truly married. She pines for you when you're not here – did you know that, Andrew?" She was talking as if Lucy wasn't there, as if, because she was just an employee at Moorgate House, her feelings and opinions mattered not.

Lucy glanced towards Andrew and to her amazement she saw that he was smiling – as if he agreed entirely with everything Nora Bruce was saying. Clarrissa too appeared to have recovered her equilibrium and was eyeing Andrew seductively.

"Just think," went on Nora Bruce softly, "if it had been you two we could all still be in London. Ah, can you picture it, Clarrissa? You and Andrew, going to theatres, parties, the two of you entertaining your friends, with Clarrissa the belle of the ball, entrancing everyone with her playing . . . And the dances you could have attended – because of course you would still be able to dance, Clarrissa; Andrew wouldn't have let you—"

It was as well that Lorn's footsteps sounded in the passage at that moment or Lucy wouldn't have been able to refrain from opening her mouth and screaming at Nora Bruce to close her poisonous lips.

To make matters worse Lorn was full of concern over Clarrissa, giving her pills to soothe her nerves, putting his arms around her reassuringly, kissing her hair, conveying his devotion to her in every way he knew how, till finally she said irritably, "Oh, I'm alright now, Lorn. Go to your place, there's a dear. Breakfast won't be worth eating if we don't have it now."

Lucy thought how appropriate was life at Moorgate House to her comparison with snakes and ladders, for no sooner had they all slid down a big slippery snake than they were climbing a ladder to loftier heights.

After breakfast Andrew caught hold of her in the hall and kissed her deeply. "Merry Christmas, darling," he murmured into the delicate shell of her ear. "I got you something when I was out yesterday. I hope you like it."

"Let me go, Andrew, someone could come out and see us."

"So what, I have every right to kiss you and the blazes with everyone. We're standing right under the mistletoe. I hung bunches of it everywhere, so be warned: that kissable little mouth of yours is going to be well and truly busy this Christmas."

He ran his hands down the sleeves of her angora dress. "Mmm, nice and soft, I love the feel of it but not so much as the feel of what's beneath it."

She looked into his smiling blue eyes and burst out laughing. "Oh, Allan, you're impossible."

"Allan is impossible, Andrew is irresistible, don't forget that, my darling Lucy."

Lucy turned away from him, feeling as if she was

caught up in a vortex of emotions from which there was no escape, whirling, whirling ever faster, helplessly spinning round, nothing making sense to her any more, and she was becoming too confused to fight back, too weary to struggle against a tide that was becoming stronger, more forceful, with every passing minute.

In the sitting room everyone was opening parcels with a merry abandon that blew away the emnity that had existed over the breakfast table. Even Lorn seemed determined to enjoy the mood of the moment and was pulling parcels from under the tree, handing them round, kissing the female recipients, and shaking hands with his brother.

A small mound of gifts remained beneath the tree, things for Meg and her husband and some for family friends. Lucy stood apart from the others, on the fringe looking on. It was Clarrissa who included her with the words, "Lucy, darling, this is from me to you." She indicated a tinsel bedecked parcel lying on the carpet. "Oh come here, do, and open it. I love this time on Christmas morning, I feel like a small girl again. . . . Oh, you sweet dear girl, I love it!" She had just opened Lucy's gift to her, a satin nightdress case with the word 'Clarrissa' embroidered on it in silk threads. "Lucy, did you make this?"

"Yes, I managed to get the material in Campbeltown. I – I hope you like it," faltered Lucy, reddening.

"Like it? Darling, I love it!" Real tears shone in the older girl's eyes and she pulled Lucy down to kiss her cheek. "You really are a dear," she murmured huskily. "To think you made this – took the time and effort to make it for a cat like me. I think I love you, Lucy Pemberton. I'm glad Lorn decided I needed a nanny." It wasn't malice but

119

a front that made her utter the last words. She squeezed Lucy's arm and turned her chair abruptly away.

Andrew was trying to muster enthusiasm over the tiepin Lucy had given him and, hiding a smile she said apologetically, "It was all I could get at the last minute. I'm sorry."

"Never mind . . . look, open this." He pushed a bulky parcel into her hands.

"I'll open it later," she whispered.

"Now," he coaxed, his smile tormenting her into submission.

For what seemed eternity she sat gazing at the oyster-coloured satin nightie and negligée nestling in folds of tissue paper, then slowly she picked up the box lid to replace it, but he stayed her: "Aren't you going to take it out – see if it's your size?" He was daring her in front of everyone and she was aware that all eyes were focused on her for the second time that morning.

"Andrew, please," she whispered. "Stop it."

"Indeed, this is all very intriguing." Lorn's voice though soft, pierced her eardrums and her whole being cringed from what his thoughts would be when he saw the flimsy provocative garments his brother had chosen for a girl who had supposedly ditched him.

Clarrissa had come over and was peering down at the exquisite garments that Lucy had hastily crushed into their box. "Very intriguing indeed." Clarrissa's voice was edged with sarcasm. "I thought you two had finished with one another! Just what's going on here I'd like to know. These are hardly the sort of things a man gives to his ex-girlfriend." For a moment she both looked and sounded furious, then she let out a peal of mischievous laughter. "Darling Lucy, don't look like that! I chose these things for you – yesterday – when we were all out shopping. Poor dear Andrew didn't know what to get any of us. Well, you know what men are! Oh, stop blushing you dear little goose – I got one too – and Mother. Andrew nearly had a fit when he saw the price of everything but as there was nothing else in the store worth the wrapping paper I asked him where his Christmas spirit was, and he jolly well had to put a face on it and stump up!"

At that everyone burst out laughing, Lucy too, in her relief at seeing a slow, almost relieved smile radiating over Lorn's face.

"Now, is that quite everyone?" Clarrissa glanced round. "No, there's still Lorn and Lucy, come on, do, I'm longing to see what surprises you two have got up your sleeves for each other."

Lorn said nothing and Lucy bent to stroke Sherry who was sniffing among the debris of wrappings littering the carpet.

"Lorn, dear, surely you haven't forgotten Miss Pemberton – and she you?" Nora Bruce looked from one to the other in genuine surprise. "But that's dreadful, really dreadful. I thought you two were getting on so well together . . . that isn't easy with Lorn, I know, but on Christmas morning of all—"

"Excuse me, I think I hear Meg," intervened Lucy hastily. "I want to be the first to wish her a Merry Christmas." She rushed out to the kitchen to hug the motherly little woman to her breast then she led her into the sitting room and in the fuss that followed everyone appeared to forget that to all intents and purposes she and Lorn had not exchanged gifts.

*   *   *

The remainder of the day passed peacefully and pleasantly. After lunch Andrew suggested a drive in his car. Nora Bruce opted out with the excuse of a headache but the rest of them piled into the big peach-coloured Mercedes, Clarrissa at the front beside Andrew because it was easier for her to get into the front passenger seat.

She had two wheelchairs: the electrically propelled one for the house and a small folding one for travelling, and it was this one that Andrew cheerily heaved into the boot before tucking his long legs in behind the driving wheel and setting off through the snow covered countryside.

Lucy sat with Lorn in the back but the seat was so wide they were able to be quite apart, hunched up against their respective corners as if they were trying desperately to escape from each other.

At the front Clarrissa laughed and joked with Andrew. She was enchanted with everything that day as Lucy had seen her on no other and was always the first to spot the various forms of wildlife they encountered on the journey: a lone heron gliding against the gold-washed sky; a red squirrel sitting under a hedge with an acorn clasped in its tiny front feet; a pair of roe deer running gracefully over a ridge, their coats like ripe chestnuts in the sun, their white rumps flashing as they went along.

Lucy sat very still and quiet in the back seat, her heart quivering with a strange mixture of gladness and sadness at the beauty of the Christmas card world. More than anything she wanted to convey her feelings to Lorn but his back was to her and she remained silent.

"What's wrong, you two?" asked Andrew at one point. "The cat got your tongues?"

"I for one am just perfectly content to enjoy the scenery," replied Lucy with dignity.

122

"Oh leave them be, Andrew," said Clarrissa. "Lorn's always in a huff about something and Lucy is a naturally quiet little thing. They are both enjoying themselves in their own way so shut up do and see which one of us is the first to spot the next thing on four legs."

"There's something over there," pointed Andrew, catching her mood. "See, running up to that tree."

Clarrissa peered from the window. "It's only a dog, lifting its leg against the tree."

"That's right and I was wrong, it's got three legs now, bet you won't spot anything as unusual as that on the rest of our travels, I'm really good at this game."

They both shrieked with glee at the nonsense and Lucy felt a bubble of mirth rising in her throat. Andrew had always been able to make her laugh – unlike – she sneaked a glance at Lorn who seemed not to have heard any of the banter but was staring out of the window as if mesmerised by the passing scenery.

Andrew stopped the car high on the cliffs and lifting Clarrissa into her chair he seized the handles and began to push her along at a breathless pace. This appeared to please her greatly and tilting her face to the sky she laughed with pure delight as her chair went bouncing along. No complaints about the cold or of the great outdoors now, she was loving every minute of it, and Lucy couldn't help thinking how mixed up everything was. She should be with Andrew, and Lorn with Clarrissa. Instead, Lorn walked by her side and Andrew had taken charge of his brother's wife. He was showing off of course and Lucy had an idea he was doing it to make her feel jealous.

She watched them together, both so alike, rather selfish

123

and spoilt, each of them expert at extracting so much from life, from people.

Lucy had never thought of Andrew as selfish until their break-up. Before that everything he did had been fine and noble in her eyes.

Oh to put the clock back! She had never known such a time, had never felt so deeply for any man till Andrew. She had ached for him every minute she was apart from him and had thought there would be nothing more wonderful than being able to spend the rest of her life with him.

The wind gusted in from the sea and she saw his fair hair ruffling, glinting like gold in the sun. She felt a sudden urge to run to him and grab him away from Clarrissa; suddenly she wanted it to be just him and her running hand in hand along the cliffs, laughing and shouting for joy, stopping every now and then to kiss, to murmur words of love.

It hurt her to see him with Clarrissa. She *was* jealous, which meant – she still loved him. The rosy glow of their yesterdays was slightly more transparent now; she was less naive and could see his faults clearer but oh! the sight of him still turned her legs to jelly! Just now he was animated and windblown, silhouetted against the sky, so tall, so handsome, so filled with laughter.

Life to Andrew was there to be enjoyed to the full, no half-measures for him, he revelled in all things pleasurable and sensual and somehow or other he didn't have to try too hard to get them. He was charismatic, magnetic, people were drawn to him, they wanted to be near him, to touch some of the magic that oozed from his every pore.

Lucy watched him and ached for him all over again. He had broken her heart but still she wanted him so badly that a little sob caught in her throat and she glanced quickly at Lorn to see if he had heard it. But he just kept walking on, his strong dark profile so set and stern he might have been a thousand miles away from her, instead of here beside her.

She wondered if he was even aware that she was here by his side. He was so strange, had been such a stranger to her since that incident in the dispensary. He had said things to her since then that she couldn't really understand. His need for her was a purely physical one – yet his words to her in the car had been full of tenderness – and longing.

He had caught her with Andrew and since then had behaved like a jealous small boy. He too was watching Andrew with Clarrissa but his eyes told her nothing and she asked herself if he was as tortured by uncertainty as she was.

She couldn't tell. He was an unfathomable depth she could never hope to reach and she wasn't sure that she wanted to try. He was such a mass of contradictions, one minute driving her out of his sight with angry words, the next standing up for her as he had done in the dining room that morning.

"Lucy." He spoke her name suddenly, his deep voice so low she thought at first she had imagined it but he said it again, not looking at her. "Lucy, I'm sorry about yesterday – I – it was seeing you with Andrew, but I had no right to judge. I've been behaving like a spoilt brat." His wide, well-shaped mouth curved into a wry grin. "You're right, I am a baby and deserve a good spanking – forgive me?"

She lifted her face and looked up, straight into his eyes and she couldn't understand why she could only utter a breathless, "Alright, Lorn," before turning away quickly from the intensity of his gaze.

All at once she felt happier, her blood coursed warmly and she was no longer aware of her cold hands. Colour flooded her cheeks and he said quietly. "God, you're a picture with the wind in your hair and the roses in your bonny face. You – you look like a little girl with your fresh smooth skin and your wee red nose all shiny like Rudolph's."

A surge of pure happiness flooded her heart. Her laugh rang out and impulsively she spread her arms as if to embrace the world. Lifting her face she saw the gulls tossing in the sky like windblown fragments of paper; she heard the surf breaking against the boulder-strewn shore and watched it foaming out over the sands like a tattered lace petticoat. It was as if she was seeing and hearing the sights and sounds of the day for the first time since waking that morning and with such blinding clarity it dazzled her. "I *feel* like a little girl, Lorn, I feel newly-born."

He stretched out his hand to her and she took it, feeling his fingers curling over hers so tightly it hurt. "Lorn, let's keep it like this," she breathed. "No more sulks – promise?"

"I promise, no more tantrums or sulks, your life is yours and if I can share just a small part of it – it's better than nothing."

He smiled at her and she was entranced for it was rare to see him so. "Thank you for the little heart," she said quietly. "I love it."

His deep brown eyes gazed into hers for a long long moment and she saw that they were flecked with amber in the sunlight. He opened his mouth as though to speak but seemed to think better of it.

Slowly he uncurled his hand from hers and stepped back

a pace. "This is how we must keep it – you're right, Lucy. I mustn't touch you again – in a way I feel I'm saying goodbye."

"Oh, Lorn, don't – please don't! You have Clarrissa, you love her, I watch you with her and I think how lucky she is to have someone who loves her so deeply and devotedly as you – she loves you too – in her own way she loves you very much."

"Yes – yes, you're right of course," he whispered, and the sun caught and broke in iridescent colours on a tear captured in his thick lashes.

"I wish someone loved me the way you do Clarrissa," she said brokenly.

"Your heart hasn't mended yet, little Lucy." It wasn't a question but a statement and she made no reply.

Andrew and Clarrissa were well ahead but now they turned.

"We're going back to the car!" cried Clarrissa. "It's freezing out here and for all the distance you two have covered you might as well not have come out at all. Oh, Andrew, don't run like that!" she protested, even while she screamed with laughter as he hurtled her back over the turf to the warmth of the car.

A few days later Lucy left with Andrew who was driving her back to England to spend the New Year with her family.

"I've been a good little boy these last few days," he told her on the journey. "I've kept Clarrissa amused – and God, she needs some amusing – I've gone to my little bed every night and never so much as looked near your room. I've done my penance, Lucy, so please, please let me have my reward. I want you back, honey."

His hand came off the gear stick and strayed to her knee. "I've got some time off for the New Year, let me come up to Yorkshire to see you."

"My parents were upset at what you did to me Andrew, they won't let you over the door."

"I can stay in a nearby hotel, we could meet every day – oh, Lucy, can't you see? For once in my life I'm not asking, I'm begging. I love you, I want to hold your perfect little body in my arms again. My spirit has been in shadow since you left me, my dearest sweet darling. These last days, near you, yet apart from you, have been torture for me. I have laughed even while my heart was breaking. Everything was a pretence, I could think of nothing but you and how I could get you to love me again."

She couldn't resist his pleas. His hand on her knee was warm, his fingers moved sensuously over her stockings. She shivered. The feel of him touching her so intimately, fascinated her. He was such a passionate man, a fire burned in him that was never fully quenched and a great deal of his thought processes were taken up with the pursuit of his pleasures.

She had been weak in so many ways where he was concerned, she had given in to his every whim until there came a point when it had seemed she had no identity of her own. That persuasive charm of his could melt any woman, and there must have been lots before her. Look at how Clarrissa was besotted by him, how could she trust a man who could so easily get anyone he wanted . . .?

"Very well, Andrew." The words were out before she could stop them. "But, I warn you now, I can't – can't . . ."

"Hush, my baby," he soothed, but he was triumphant. "You may feel now you can't give yourself to me completely – but in time you will. You can't fight it forever, honey, not if you love me. And you do, you do, Lucy."

Chapter Fourteen

Jessie MacSporran was standing outside the Ardben Post Office as the mail van drew up in a flurry of diesel fumes. The driver's door opened and Hugh Patterson, the postman, went round to the back of the vehicle to bring out a bundle of mail and a couple of unplucked chickens, which one of the farmers had given him to hand in to the postmistress.

"You're late today, Hugh," observed Jessie, peering over her spectacles at him in a questioning manner.

"Ay, the mist was bad in one or two places," he nodded in explanation. "I'm here now though and Jock Cameron asked me to give you these birds. I must be getting on . . . though mind . . ." he cocked his head and grinned at her cheekily, "a cup of tea wouldn't go amiss. It's been a long haul and I need something to cheer me up."

"Ach, alright," Jessie acceded kindly. "You always were a terrible man for your tea, but in this weather it's understandable. Come away inside and I'll put the kettle on."

Hugh emerged from the post office just as Lucy was climbing down the steps of the bus with her cases. "Here, lassie, let me help you with these," he offered courteously.

130

"There's another one yet to come," Lucy told him, and he disappeared up the aisle of the bus, pausing on the way back with the case to have a word with the driver. The men obviously knew one another well and were soon engaged in animated conversation.

Lucy knew the ways of country people; time didn't mean as much to them as it did to city dwellers but she didn't mind having to wait for her case. It gave her a chance to take stock of her surroundings and she stood outside the bus, breathing deeply of the sea air while she gazed around her, eagerly drinking in the wild beauty of Kintyre.

She felt as if she had been away for weeks, had never believed she could have longed so much to get back to this place that had so captured her heart from the first moment she saw it. She felt as if she had come home and her eyes were filled with quiet satisfaction as she drank it all in. Not that there was all that much to see at this particular moment. The mist had rolled in from the sea, damp and grey, shrouding the hills, lying over the horizon like a blanket. It was as it had been when first she had set foot on Kintyre soil and she felt it was right and appropriate it should be so again.

"You're back then, lassie?" acknowledged Jessie, beaming at Lucy. "It's nice to see you again and just a pity the weather didn't see fit to give you a better welcome."

Lucy's heart sang and she thought: Yes, Jessie, I'm back, back to the land where folk never hurry and can always spare the time to stop and chat for a while.

"Ay well, you'll not have to hoof it this time," Jessie said, with the assurance of one who knew just what was going on in her immediate vicinity. "The doctor is waiting for you yonder in front of the tackle shop." She turned

131

her attention once more on Lucy. "Have you had a good time over New Year then?"

"Lovely, thanks, Jessie," said Lucy brightly.

"Ach well, it was quiet here, we don't have the bright lights and noise in these parts but there were a few sore heads in the village just the same . . ." Here she threw a meaningful glance at Hugh who was just emerging from the bus. "And still are by the look of some of them!"

Lucy smiled in delight. Bright lights and noise! It was obvious that Jessie considered anything that was outwith the boundaries of her experience to be somewhat on the wild side.

The children were coming out of school, drifting along in small groups, the murmur of their voices almost drowned by a swarm of gulls swooping and diving noisily overhead.

"Hallo, Miss Pemberton," the children called, raising their hands in greeting, and Lucy waved back, a warmth coming into her heart at the sight of the rosy faces smiling shyly at her as they passed. She knew most of them by name now and felt a surge of joy in that knowledge, her memory taking her back to the day she had first set foot in this place of wide spaces.

She hadn't known a soul then, had been torn apart by feelings of desolation and loneliness. Now all that was in the past. She had been made welcome by the people of Ardben and felt that she belonged here now.

Hugh was gathering up her cases, announcing his intention of carrying them for her to the car, and when she protested he shook his head and said firmly, "Now, now, there is always time in my book to give a helping hand to a bonny lassie."

With a wink at Jessie he walked with Lucy to the car and before Lorn was halfway out of it he was shouting a friendly greeting. "It's yourself then, Dr Campbell. How are you? Done in by the look of you! You would be better off being a postman or some such thing, or else you could send all the sick folk out of the village and apply for healthy ones to take their place." He chuckled. On second thoughts, you would have so much time on your hands you would maybe find yourself out of a job so it might be better to keep things as they are for a while!"

Over the roof of the car Lucy looked at Lorn and he caught her glance and smiled.

Hugh was throwing the cases into the boot with more zest than care and when he had finished doing that he stood by the door till Lucy had climbed in. "There you are now, all present and correct. Just be minding the hem of your coat and I'll be giving the door a good wallop to make sure it's shut right."

There was an almighty thud that made her shudder and Lorn, climbing in behind the steering wheel, grinned at her expression. "Hugh is the perfect gentleman but he has no respect for the modern motor car, having been brought up in a smiddy where horses held sway over everything."

They pulled away from the post office, waving at Jessie and Hugh who were standing in the doorway, watching as they drove away.

It wasn't yet dark and Lucy settled into her seat to look from the window. Some of the children hadn't gone straight home from school but had scrambled down to the shore to indulge in a bit of beachcombing, small groups of them poking and probing with great optimism among

133

the debris left by the tide, all of them very purposeful and silent as they went along.

Lucy had been quick to notice this restraint of theirs. Even when they were playing they could do it and enjoy it without having to yell noisily at one another. There was a reserve about them which she found endearing and when several of them looked up and waved at the car she gave a little chuckle of appreciation.

"You're fond of the bairnies," observed Lorn.

"I love them," she returned simply. "They're the nicest children you could wish to meet anywhere."

Her words were met with silence and she turned her attention from the window to scrutinise him. Hugh was right. He was 'done in' looking. His face was white and strained, his shoulders were sagging slightly, as if he was carrying a burden that was too much for him to bear.

A stab of dread went through her. He had had much the same appearance on their first meeting, but gradually, as the weeks passed, he seemed to have shaken off some of his worries. He had looked less strained, had been more sure of himself, he had carried himself like a man who faced the world with a sense of confidence.

True he had been moody with her, but that was something different to the despair she had sensed in him at the beginning. Now it was back. She could feel it enshrouding him, twisting like a knife into a wound that was already raw, so strong she could feel the waves of it reaching out to her, making her shiver.

"How is Clarrissa?" she asked warily, feeling that she was treading on delicate ground even though the question she asked was simple and natural.

A muscle quivered in his jaw, he gritted his teeth and

said flatly, "She's – well – you'll see for yourself soon enough."

The few stilted words filled her with more dread than any detailed description. She knew – she knew as sure as fate, that Clarrissa was back to square one: acting up, throwing tantrums, testing everyone's nerves to the limit.

In a moment of panic she wondered if she could face it all again – as it had been at the start: Clarrissa – catty, spoiled, spiteful, difficult and uncooperative. Yet, even as she doubted her limits of endurance she resolved that she wasn't going to be beaten by Clarrissa, or anyone else, and her firm little chin went out determinedly.

She had managed before, she would do so again; nothing was going to take away her joyous feelings at coming back, no one was going to rob her of the warm deep sense of tranquil happiness she was experiencing at this moment, simply because she was back in Kintyre, going back to Moorgate House – with Lorn at her side.

She had missed him. Before her departure to England they had barely spoken two words – yet – she hardly wanted to admit to herself how much she had longed for his strong, overpowering presence, his eyes looking at her, filled with so many strange expressions that she couldn't even begin to fathom.

As if reading her thoughts his hand came out and took hers. It was warm and firm. "It's – been strange without you – I'm glad you're home."

Home! He considered Moorgate House as her home now. The thought poured more happiness into that which was already there.

"Have you enjoyed your holiday?" he asked, and it was her turn to tense up.

"It was lovely to see my parents," she answered, and said nothing more on the subject. It had been wonderful to be home with her mother and father in the big rambling farmhouse in Yorkshire. But Andrew hadn't been wonderful. To begin with it had been fine. She had gone to meet him several times, feeling guilt in her because she went without her parents' knowledge. Andrew had been very gentle with her at first, gentle and patient, as if they were just embarking on a romance and were getting to know one another. But he hadn't been able to keep that up for long, his sexual voracity had seen to that. Foolishly she had accepted an invitation to dine with him in his hotel room. "Soft lights and music, my darling, and you and me. I promise you I won't do anything to cause you alarm."

He had chosen to stay in a hotel well outside the vicinity of Lucy's village, telling her he had done so for her sake. "I wouldn't want you bumping into anyone who might run off and tell your parents the big bad wolf is back in town," he had laughed.

She had known full well that these weren't the reasons why he had picked the hotel. He had chosen it because it was the most modern in the area and Andrew liked his comforts.

The room he was in was big and spacious, with a phone, colour television and a bathroom en-suite. The meal had been perfect and he had set out to be the perfect host, charming and gracious, attending her every need, holding her hand over the table while he paid her compliments.

She had felt pampered and special. They had drunk ice-cold champagne, chinking their glasses together, giggling when the bubbles tickled their noses. But he didn't stop at one bottle, he had ordered another and had kept topping up her glass, pressing her to drink, despite her protests. He had taken far too much himself, his face becoming flushed, his eyes over bright. She hadn't wanted the lovemaking to start, knowing from experience where it would lead, where it always led with Andrew, and she had risen from the table to pick her coat up from the bed.

"You're surely not going?" he had asked incredulously. "You don't really think I'm going to let you walk out of here just like that!"

"I am going, Andrew," she had returned evenly. "It's been lovely, I've enjoyed our evening but it's over now and I'd like to go home."

"Oh, would you now?" he had returned coldly. "And do you really think I'm going to be damned fool enough to let you walk out of here without so much as a goodnight kiss?" Like a tiger he had sprung at her, pinning her arms, roughly forcing his kisses on her, bruising her mouth. "I love you, Lucy!" he cried harshly. "And you love me, you know you do. If you feel for me the way you always said you did you will give me anything – forgive me anything!"

Panic gripped her then and her heart hammered into her throat. His blue eyes were glazed with desire and she had wondered then if he was seeing her as Lucy Pemberton – or as just another girl to be vanquished, and then, having conquered her he would grow tired of her . . . of any woman.

It was the challenge that excited him. The idea of that had never entered her head till then, she had been too blinded by love to see it before. In those violent moments of struggling to release herself from his crushing embraces the final veil lifted from her eyes and she saw him for what he was: a pampered, pleasure-seeking playboy, who thought women had been put on earth for his benefit alone.

"You don't love me!" she had blazed at him. "You don't love anyone but yourself! You lie all the time to get your own way – your very name was a lie to me! Can I call you Allan tonight? Or would you prefer Andrew? Or some other trumped up title you think might impress? Do all your women call you by different names, I wonder?"

"I don't have other women, only you – oh my sweet, my honey, you're so lovely. I dream about you every night, of possessing you, you've become an obsession with me!"

"Let me go, Andrew, please!" she cried. "Don't allow this to happen – in future, when I think of you, I – I want my thoughts of you to be happy ones, I would hate us to part in anger."

But he wasn't listening, he was growing furious at her now, a rage that had lent him even more strength. His fingers on her arms were like bands of steel. He began ripping off his shirt; his bronzed body big and terrifying, looming above her, blotting out the light, the muscles of his shoulders rippling.

"Andrew, I warn you, I want you to let go of me!" she had panted.

"Oh no, tonight you're mine, Lucy," he had gritted. "Don't struggle, it only makes it all the more exciting. You surely know that by now."

There was no shred of gentleness in him at this point, he was brutal and surly, hurting her, giving thought to no one but himself. She had screamed then and she had gone on screaming, louder and louder.

In a sweating fury he had drawn away from her and had slapped her on the face, from side to side, over and over, but still she kept on screaming till he cursed and pushed her away, his broad chest heaving.

"Bitch! Little bitch!" he had fumed, the words slurred with drink. "I've wined you and dined you and this is my thanks."

Sobbing, feeling sickened, humiliated and soiled, her face burning where his hands had struck it unmercifully, she had pushed her arms frantically into her coat, wanting only to get out of the room, her whole being consumed with self-loathing for being so foolish as to allow herself to get into this situation in the first place.

"We're through, Andrew! I told you that before and this time I mean it!" she had flung at him. "To think once I thought you loved me – that I loved you. I would have given you the world if I could but what have you ever given me but heartache? Now that I think of it, you kept telling me you loved me but never once did you ever mention marriage . . ."

"Marriage!" He had thrown the word back at her derisively. "You're living in the past, Lucy darling. Nowadays a chaste kiss doesn't mean a wedding ring will follow. I'm enjoying myself as I am – why should I marry? I can get what I want without tying myself down like that."

"Exactly! But you won't get it from me," she told him coldly. "We're finished, Andrew Allan Campbell!"

He had laughed mockingly. "We'll see about that, sweetheart. Remember, I'll be going home to bonny Scotland quite often, so keep your bed warm for me – that is if you're not too busy warming big brother's! He's got his beady eye on you, Clarrissa's got hers on me. We could all have a fine time playing postman's knock in and out of each other's rooms."

"You're a despicable, uncouth beast!" she had stormed and had gladly left the scene, his derisive laughter ringing in her ears as she fled along the corridor.

Chapter Fifteen

Now, sitting beside Lorn, her thoughts reddened her face and she was glad that he was too intent on driving the car through the mist-bound roads to notice anything unusual.

She was therefore all the more taken aback when he said without any preliminary, "How is that bruised little heart of yours, Lucy?"

"I don't remember telling you that my heart was anything else but perfectly sound," she answered, in a startled rush.

"You didn't have to — I knew — just as I also know the ache has now gone out of it."

She said nothing, relieved that they had turned in through the big wooden gates and she was able to make the pretence of searching in her bag for her comb.

She held her breath as the car went up the drive, and there the old house stood, solid and reassuring, its ivy-covered walls giving the impression that they would go on standing forever, no matter how battered by storm and time.

Lorn stopped the car, and going round to the back he retrieved her luggage from the boot. "This time I don't have to tell you where to go," he told her with a smile. "You're home, Lucy, and your room is waiting."

With a surge of youthful high spirits she ran into the house and straight upstairs to her room to throw her hat in the air in a gluttony of joy. She stood, her hands clasped to her chin as she gazed about her, adoring the sight of the big double bed with its rose-sprigged eiderdown; the antique dresser; the chintz armchairs with their big fluffy cushions.

The firescreen had been removed from the hearth and a welcoming fire leapt up the chimney. On the mantelpiece sat a vase of golden daffodils and tightly-curled pink tulips.

Lorn came in with the cases and she turned to him. "Thank you – oh thank you for everything – especially the flowers."

"I got them in Campbeltown to welcome you back," he said with embarrassed brusqueness. "It's too early yet for them to be showing in the garden."

"Oh, Lorn." Impulsively she threw her arms round his neck and kissed him. He stood quite still, gazing down at her and Lucy felt a strange shiver run down her spine. She wanted to turn away from his deep compelling eyes but instead she returned his look as of one hypnotised. He made no move to touch her, his mouth was set, tense almost, a muscle in his lean jaw was working as if he was having to exercise all his self-control not to make a move towards her.

A tide of emotions swelled in her breast and though he did not so much as lay a finger on her she felt as if she was lying in the powerful circle of his arms.

"Don't do these things to me, Lucy." His lips formed the words haltingly. "Before you went away I made a promise not to touch you again but I am very much flesh and blood and you are tempting me beyond bearing. It would be a very easy thing for me to lock us both into this room and I couldn't promise to answer for the consequences of that."

The blood drained from her face and her heart fluttered like that of an imprisoned bird. "You wouldn't dare do such a thing," she said, her throat suddenly tight because more than anything else in the world she wanted him to take her in his arms and kiss her until the world spun crazily.

His eyes were still holding hers and she saw fire in them. "Oh, wouldn't I? Are you asking me to prove my manhood, Lucy?"

Anger swamped her suddenly. Anger at him, anger at herself for having been weak enough to want his kisses, to be held by him, loved by him, till she was beyond caring about anything – anyone . . .

"Oh, so it runs in the family," she said with defensive coolness. "Am I to take it that you are like your brother Andrew? Strutting around, the stud of the stables?" The words were out before she could prevent them. She stopped short in her tirade, appalled at herself and frightened at the icy glitter that had crept into his eyes.

He came slowly towards her and stood towering above her, big and powerful and somehow frightening. "So, you compare me to Andrew." His voice was as brittle as hoar frost. "In that case perhaps you expect me to behave like him. However, I'm not going to. Apparently he needs no excuses to come into this house and kiss a girl he was supposed to have finished with. I have an excuse: it's New Year, a time for exchanging greetings – and kisses . . ."

His arms came out to crush her in a fierce embrace. Lucy struggled but his grip on her tightened further till she was pressed against his hard taut body. His head

143

came down and his lips claimed hers, forcing her own apart, his tongue probing till it found hers.

A tidal wave of sensual excitement submerged her, her legs felt weak and trembled beneath her. For a moment she could do nothing, so helpless with longing was she, then she forgot everything and kissed him back, melted into him, her body a supple soft unresisting thing with no will left in it to fight, to draw back, to deny him anything he asked of her.

Deeper and deeper they kissed, their bodies moulding together till it seemed they were of the same pulsing fiery flesh. With a helpless little moan she felt herself drowning in a world of warm, beating, desire, that rushed through her veins like a river of white hot fire, the feeling growing more intense as she felt his mounting passion, heard his groans of longing deep in his throat.

Then abruptly he pushed her away. His breath was harsh and fast as he said in a voice that was slightly shaky, "I can't say I'm sorry – it was too wonderful for that. I'm not going to ask you to forgive me either – for – if I'm not very much mistaken – I think I can safely say you enjoyed it as much as I did."

Trembling, she sank onto the bed. "Please, please – will you leave me now. I – I must unpack."

He came back to look down at her and now his eyes were tender as he cupped her chin in his hand and bent to kiss her gently. "Happy New Year, Lucy," he said huskily. "I hope it will be a wonderful one for you."

Reluctantly he backed away from her. "I must go down now. Elspeth has come in early to help me make up prescriptions. Nora will have made some tea. If you go down now it will be fine and hot. Clarrissa is resting but will be wanting you to dress her for dinner as usual.

144

If you don't feel up to it just yet, Nora has said she will do it."

She passed a hand over her eyes and shook her head. "It's – it's alright, I'll manage. I'll have that cup of tea and a shower to freshen me up – and then I'll be ready for anything."

"You'll have to be," he murmured quietly, in control of himself again, polite, somewhat distant – as if that which had just passed between them had never been. But at the door he turned and said, "When you were away this house was empty. You have brought life back to it, Lucy – and I feel as if I have come alive again too."

He ran downstairs and Lucy lay back, every nerve in her body quivering with the awareness of what had just taken place, yet her mind too numbed by the experience to fully grasp what was happening to her. As if in protest she shook her head from side to side. She mustn't think of Lorn as anything else but her employer, she had to forget what had happened between them – yet, even as she told herself these things she knew that in the nights to come she would go over every little detail of the interlude, remember the overwhelming excitement of his lips on hers, his passion, his hard, demanding maleness . . .

With an effort she forced herself to get up on her feet and set about the business of unpacking. She was a nurse, she told herself, a companion; she was here at Moorgate House to do a job. Nora Bruce was waiting to serve tea, Clarrissa was waiting to be dressed, and she would have to behave normally, though everything in her ached to know again the sweet ecstasy of Lorn's strong arms around her, holding her close.

Chapter Sixteen

Lucy's premonitions about Clarissa soon proved to be only too accurate. She had been difficult before, now she was impossible. She threw temper tantrums at the least provocation; stormed; wept; often she refused to get out of bed and demanded drugs to make her sleep.

She wouldn't go out and complained loudly about being bored indoors. Food was left untouched and that which was sent to her in her bedroom was undoubtedly fed to Sherry who grew fatter while his mistress grew thinner and listless.

She seemed bent on making Lorn's life a hell. Previously she had taunted and teased him with innuendoes, now she came right out with the things that were on her mind, if not in front of the other members of the household, then shouting so loudly at him that everyone heard anyway.

A fortnight after Lucy's return she heard them from her bedroom. It was one of the worst rows yet, with Clarissa screaming at her husband, "Why, why don't you divorce me? I want to be free of you, Lorn! Why do you keep hanging on? Why, why, why?"

And Lorn: "You need someone to look after you and I'm damned well going to do that if it kills me!"

"And it might, Lorn, it just might! It's your conscience

isn't it? Your guilty little conscience! You made me like this! Half a woman! You made me have that baby because you wanted an heir, someone to carry on the good old family name. You were in cloud cuckoo land. A loving wife and mother. A son to follow in Daddy's footsteps! Healing the sick, bowing and scraping. Oh, everybody worships Dr Lorn Campbell! They don't know how selfish you are!"

"You don't know what you're saying, Clarrissa, you're overwrought. Please, darling, stop it!" Lorn's voice was growing louder and Lucy could just picture the scene: Clarrissa lying in bed, white-faced with fury, yelling all that cruel abuse at an equally white-faced Lorn trying to keep in control, desperately trying to keep the cork on all his suppressed emotions.

"Oh, I don't know what I'm saying now!" Clarrissa's voice had risen to such a pitch it seemed to reverberate round and round the house, terrifying in all its scornful fury. "You'll be saying next that I am mad. That would be good! A good way to get me out of your sight and forget about me, forget what you've done to me! Lorn, please . . ." Her voice had dropped slightly. "Please let Mother take me back to London – she could look after me just as well there as here."

"How? Tell me that, Clarrissa. I've poured thousands into this house, converting it for you, giving you things, doing everything to make life easier for you! I can't afford to do anything more and I certainly can't afford to keep you and your mother in a flat in London. You would always want more, more than I could ever give you."

"Oh, you've got all the trump cards haven't you?" Her voice was like steel, cold and menacing. "Casting up! The big man. Make life easier for me indeed. Ha!

147

That's a laugh – only I don't find it particularly funny. But I tell you this, Lorn: I'll get away without you and your money. You see if I don't!"

"As you like, Clarrissa! You've always had your own way, there's no reason why you should stop now."

A door banged, then there was silence. Lucy found that she was sitting on the edge of her bed, her face in her hands, the tears pouring unchecked down her cheeks. She could never have believed that anyone could be so venomous and as cruel as Clarrissa if she hadn't heard the words for herself.

How could anyone say such things to another human being? Especially to a man so considerate and as patient as Lorn. Perhaps that was the trouble: he was too patient, too tolerant; if he turned on his wife and gave her as good as he got it might do her the world of good.

She was taunting him, goading him into it, as if she wanted him to lash out at her. Lucy knew that only some terrible force of willpower kept him from doing so and she marvelled at his strength of mind, his continuing loyalty to a wife who scorned him.

Sitting there on her bed, Lucy realised that the only reason she stayed on at Moorgate House was Lorn. She knew he needed her badly, perhaps because she always tried to bring a sense of normality into an abnormal situation. He was reaching out to her more and more, trusting her, confiding little things to her about his work, about himself. No one else in the house appeared even mildly interested in his affairs and she couldn't desert him, couldn't leave him to a stark reality that held nothing for him.

Day by day the atmosphere in the house grew more tense,

more oppressive. Even Nora Bruce, that cool pillar of composure, was showing strain. She was uneasy-looking, as if she too had lost control of the situation and didn't know how to cope with her own daughter any more. She had put the match to the fire and now it was out of her control.

In desperation Lucy spoke to Meg about it. Meg sat down heavily and shook her white head sadly, though anger glinted out of her eyes. "Ach, lassie lassie, it's always the same after his lordship goes away – only this is the worst I've seen it."

"You mean . . . ?"

"Andrew, ay, I mean him alright. Up until Christmas he wasn't near the place for nearly a year, then he has to come back with all his fancy ways, all the kind of laughing and the talking that Clarrissa laps up like a kitten laps cream. He brings memories back with him – of the kind of life she had loved before the baby was born. She can't adjust like a normal lassie would; spoiled all her life, tended hand and foot like a princess."

Meg's lips folded into a tight line of disapproval. "I blame that mother of hers – she drove her own man to the grave you know – made him work his fingers to the bone so that they could have standards far above their means. Everything had to be of the best for her daughter – she had her sights set on poor Lorn from the start, saw him as a good catch, never dreaming how it would all end, not looking far enough ahead to the reality of what it would be like for Clarrissa as the wife of a country doctor. She only saw the money side of it and was annoyed at her daughter for gadding about with other men. But Clarrissa didn't need to get her hooks into Lorn to catch him: he was enchanted by her from the start, for though I say it myself she has the looks that would take the feet from under any man – and by God, she swept Lorn off his so fast he didn't have so much as a wee toe left to stand on!"

"But she's so cruel to him! Surely if she loved him she could at least show him some compassion?"

"Loved him? That vain wee madam never loved anyone but herself! It's money she loves – ay – and Lorn had plenty of that, for he was always a careful one – canny we say here. His lordship on the other hand was always a one for the pennies burning holes in his pocket. Throws money about like water – just so long as he gets a good return for it, you might say. Oh ay, he'll give you a shilling with one hand and hold out the other for a pound."

Lucy knew only too well what Meg meant. Money in Andrew's wallet was there to be spent – just so long as he got most of the end profits. He had proved that to her in the hotel room with his lavish show of food and drink – a spread for which he felt he ought to be well rewarded. "Oh, Meg," she said wearily. "How does Lorn put up with it?"

Meg reached over the table and patted the girl's hand. "Penance my lassie, he's paying his penance. He knows if he ever stops paying – ever lets go – well then – that pair would just go up in smoke. They've got fuel and enough for their tongues now, but let poor Lorn say one word in self-defence and they've got him where they want him, at their level, snarling, back-biting, never letting up for a minute. The only thing he's got left is his dignity and pray God he keeps it."

She looked at Lucy's troubled face. "You've been kind to him, my lassie," she said gently. "I've watched you doing little things for him that bring a light into his eyes. There was a time when the joy of living was never out of them . . . Now . . ." She spread her hands expressively and Lucy grabbed them and held them tight.

"Meg, I'm going to have a right good talk with Clarrissa, try to make her see sense, I think it's time somebody did."

Meg rose wearily. "You can try, lass, you can try, but don't expect miracles."

Lucy spoke to Clarrissa that afternoon. She was lying in her room, delicate and languid-looking among her satin cushions. Lucy said hesitantly, "I think it's time you and I had a little chat, Clarrissa."

She turned her head impatiently on the pillow and said rudely, "Oh go away, Lucy, can't you see I'm resting?"

Lucy's chin went up. Firmness was what Clarrissa needed. Lorn had said that, and Lucy had proved it for herself on more than one occasion. "Oh stop behaving like a spoiled child!" she snapped. "We're all sick to death of your constant moaning and wailing. Starve yourself, shut yourself away, but do it peaceably so that no one else is forced to suffer with you!"

Clarrissa's head came round sharply to stare at the younger girl in disbelief. "Who the hell do you think you are telling *me* what to do? Don't you ever forget you're being paid to act as my nursemaid!"

"It takes more than money to make me do what I'm doing for a girl who thinks only of herself continually and the hell with the rest of the world. Listen, Clarrissa," she sat down on the edge of the bed and though her heart was pumping too fast she went on determinedly, "you don't know just how lucky you are, it's all been made easy for you. I've seen people in the same position as yourself, living in such impoverished circumstances they don't know what it is to be warm in winter. Some have to stay in bed because it's the only way they can keep warm; they can't get outside at all because of stairs and what have you. I've seen bedridden young women in hospital whiling away their weary hours by making things for people they consider worse off than themselves."

She gave a short little laugh. "Can you believe that? No, I don't think you can. As far as you're concerned you're the only person in the world with the ill-fortune to have ended up in a wheelchair. Do you ever think of the children . . .?"

"Alright, alright!" The cry of protest burst from the older girl's lips and she put a hand over her eyes. "You've made your point! Don't go on, I can't bear it, for God's sake. Oh you're right, Lucy Pemberton – I am spoilt and selfish – but . . ." She turned away again, her face against her shoulder. "I'm so unhappy, you don't know how much."

"Don't I? We all know it and you're spreading it around like a contagious disease. It's time you snapped out of it. You make your husband's life a misery with your constant accusations, yet he goes on putting up with it – how I'll never understand. He's good and decent and he works so hard for you. Any other man would have walked out on you long ago – or let you go your own wilful way.

"But he won't leave you, he has a strength that forces him on and on till one day he will either snap or drop. I tell you this, Clarrissa, in the end he might be the only one left that will be here to put up with you! I'm sick to the teeth of it all! Several times I've been on the point

152

of packing and getting out, then I think: tomorrow she might be a little better, but you never are and I'm at the end of my tether with you."

Clarrissa looked at her with disbelieving eyes then reaching out a trembling hand she clutched Lucy's arm. "Oh no, don't say that, don't go, Lucy, please, I've grown used to having you here. I never thought I'd ever admit that but it's true. At first I didn't want you here, and later I didn't want to hurt Mother by letting her see I preferred your company to hers, so I kept on being catty to you – but Lorn was right, I needed somebody young – I need you, Lucy."

Lucy felt light-headed with triumph and more than a little relief at Clarrissa's reaction to the lecture she had just received. "If the day comes, Clarrissa," she forced herself to say firmly, "when you begin to realise that people need to feel needed in return, then you will have taken a step in the right direction. Try it with your husband: you couldn't start with a finer, more deserving person. And there endeth the first lesson, thank heaven. I feel like a hundred years old talking to you like this, so how about getting back to normal and start by giving me my orders for the rest of the day?"

Some days later a puzzled Lorn spoke to Lucy in the kitchen. "A little bird has been working miracles in this house," he said with a warm smile of bemusement. "Clarrissa isn't exactly singing like a skylark but she's stopped having tantrums and she actually asked just now if you would get her ready to go out." He laid his hand over hers. "Thank you, little Lucy Pemberton, I don't know how you did it but I do know it's you I have to thank."

Over the next weeks Clarrissa changed dramatically. She no longer raved and shouted, instead she was the complete opposite, with a quietness about her that was almost eerie. Obediently she arose each morning; she allowed Lucy to take her out; she began to show an interest in food; she made no murmur of protest or argument about the things that had once so annoyed her.

At first Lucy thought it might be just another tactic, a new way to gain attention. But gradually she came to the realisation that the older girl wasn't putting on an act; was in fact, deeply and helplessly unhappy. She was like a little girl, clinging more and more to Lucy, turning away from her mother to such a noticeable extent that for the first time Lucy began to feel sorry for Nora Bruce.

Spring came to Kintyre with a suddenness that was breathtaking. It had rained for weeks, with the burns foaming down from the hills, swelling the rivers that flooded in spate into the sea. When the sodden earth could absorb no more moisture, the fields became flooded and filled with seagulls, squabbling like noisy children in paddling pools.

The clocks were put forward to British summertime and it was as if someone somewhere in the land had flicked a switch from winter to spring. Sunshine cascaded over the countryside, daffodils swayed in the breezes; the skies became big and wide and blue; birds sang from every tree; buds grew fat and shiny and ready to burst into flower.

Lucy took Clarrissa for long walks and they would stop on the clifftops to look towards blue hills basking on far horizons. Lucy, unable to help herself, exclaimed ecstatically over the beauty of the awakening world and gradually her mood rubbed off on Clarrissa who sat one day, staring at the foaming surf below, as if she was seeing the sea for the first time.

Her hands were folded peacefully in her lap and her lustrous eyes were bright with tears. "You know, Lucy," she murmured, "I think – if things had been different – I might have grown to love this place."

Lucy crouched down in front of her and took her hands. "Things can be different if you let them, Clarrissa, and you will, given time you will."

But the older girl shook her head. "I wish my philosophy was as simple as yours, Lucy, but I'm much too complicated a brat and it's too late now to change what I am, but I'm trying, oh God, if only you knew how hard I'm trying." She sighed. "If only I didn't have to go into this silly nursing home! I really shouldn't have listened to you, Lucy. If I didn't have to go away I might really have enjoyed this marvellous beginning to summer."

Lucy said nothing. She had somehow managed to persuade Clarrissa to go into hospital to have further investigations made on her condition, urging her to think positive with a view to recovery in the future and in a burst of optimism Clarrissa had agreed.

Lorn had been delighted and had made the arrangements for his wife to be admitted to a nursing home which was situated some considerable distance from Ardben.

"I'll come with you darling, of course," Nora Bruce had said determinedly when she heard of the plans.

"Oh, Mother, there's no need!" Clarrissa had returned crossly. "I'll only be away for a week or two and I'll have Lucy. You can stay here till I come back."

"Here? In this place! All alone without you!" Nora

Bruce made it sound as if she was being abandoned on the moon. "Oh no, darling, I must be with you. I can stay in a nearby hotel and come to see you every day."

"Oh, Mother, must you really follow me everywhere?" Clarrissa had cried, raising her eyes to the ceiling in exasperation. But in the end, she had given in, simply because to refuse would have meant listening forever to her mother's arguments and reasons for and against.

On the day of her departure Lorn took Clarrissa's hands in his and bent to kiss her. "You'll be alright, darling, I'll phone every night and I'll come down to see you every Sunday."

"Really, Lorn, you don't have to do that, I'm not going away forever. I wish to God you would all stop treating me like a baby . . ." She stopped short and had the grace to look ashamed. "I know, it's because I behave like one. I'm sorry, do come if you can – and – you'll be alright, Meg will see to that."

Lucy was taking Lorn's car because it was roomy enough for Clarrissa to stretch out in the back. In the hall he handed her the keys. They were alone; Clarrissa and her mother were making their way to the car parked at the door.

He smiled ruefully. "The house is going to seem strange without Clarrissa's voice – and . . ." He reached out and clasped both her hands in his. His throat was working and he breathed huskily, "God, how I'm going to miss you, your quick step in the hall; your wee voice humming in the kitchen; the sunshine of you filling all the corners. What am I going to do without you, Lucy? Tell me."

It was just before morning surgery and he was wearing

his white coat. He looked pure and young with his newly-shaven face fresh and clean under his thick curling brown hair, the unruly lock of it straying over his brow. She felt such an urge to reach out and touch it that the only way she could stop herself from doing so was to turn her eyes away from him.

The grip on her hands tightened. "You are standing against the sun Lucy Pemberton, and your hair is a halo round your head with little threads of it like spun gold, brighter even than sunlight . . ."

She tore her hands away. "Don't, please don't! Will you come now and lift Clarrissa into the car? I don't want her to be uncomfortable in any way. I have arranged some nice soft cushions at her back so she should survive alright till we get there."

"You are making a good job of what you came here to do, Lucy – I'm sorry, I almost broke my promise just now – but – the only reason I trusted myself to touch you was because I know that, in a few minutes, you will be walking away from me."

She didn't answer, she couldn't, and without a word she followed him out to the sundrenched garden. Above her the gulls were wheeling; a curlew bubbled out its spring song in some hidden hollow; the breezes were bringing the fragrance of the moors to her nostrils; lambs were bleating from the fields; a chaffinch trilled joyously nearby; the flower beds were ablaze with tulips and sweet-scented hyacinths.

She reached out and touched the fat sticky buds on a low-hanging branch of horse chestnut before turning abruptly to hurry to the car, every fibre in her longing to stay and savour the pure joy of the warm sun on her face and the sights and sounds that surrounded the sturdy fortress of Moorgate House . . . but most of all, when she looked in the driving mirror and saw Lorn standing alone, his hand raised in farewell . . . she wanted to turn and run – run like a deer – back to him and all he stood for.

Chapter Seventeen

Barely a fortnight had passed and Clarrissa was bored and irritable. Lucy couldn't really blame her for this as she had to spend much of her time in bed owing to a severe head cold which made her sneeze and snuffle, grumble and complain, and generally feel sorry for herself.

The assessment was taking longer than any of them had anticipated. Several specialists had come to see her and had ordered that various tests be carried out, including visits to the X-ray department, and blood samples which Clarrissa hated.

Outside, the sun continued to spill its rays over the land, which made the situation even more unbearable as, contrarily, she now hankered after the outdoor world.

Lucy read to her; devised various games for her to play; talked to her and generally tried to make the long hours pass as pleasantly as possible. Nora Bruce came every day, allowing Lucy to get outside for an hour or two, and Lorn had visited twice, though Lucy hadn't seen him, one half of her longing for a glimpse of him, the other telling herself sternly that it was only right that husband and wife should be alone together.

She found herself fretting for just a sight of him and on his second visit she arrived back at the home in time to see him driving Clarrissa's little car out of the gates. She stood for a long moment, drinking in that brief glimpse of him at the wheel till he was just a black dot in the distance.

Stop it, stop it, Lucy Pemberton, she scolded herself. It's compassion you feel for him. What girl wouldn't be sorry for a man in his position?

She was torn in two. Each night she lay in bed, recalling everything that had happened between them, the things he had said; that time in the dispensary when his kisses had burned into her; the interlude in the car when he had told her he wanted to hold her in his arms forever. It wasn't fair of him to say such things, to take advantage of her vulnerability. He was a man denied of physical intimacy with his wife, so what more natural that he should seek it elsewhere? It wasn't because he was particularly fond of her or anything like that. He would have tried his luck with any reasonably attractive girl who was under the same roof as him and who was so available.

Men were like that. In the next thought she told herself he was not like other men; certainly not like his brother, Andrew, who wouldn't have given her a moment's peace knowing she slept just a few paces away from him.

Lorn had never once given her any reason to feel such unease. She had never had to lock her door against him, yet Andrew, on the first night of his Christmas holiday at Moorgate House, after the lies, the deceit and the break-up, had had the nerve to expect admittance to her room.

Andrew! How strange that she had barely given him a thought since New Year and on the few occasions that she allowed her mind to stray to that time she shuddered with revulsion and felt uneasy as she wondered when he would pop up again, flashing his charm around, smiling his winning smile, talking his fancy talk.

160

It was all such a façade and she wondered how she had ever been taken in by him. She had been blind with infatuation. After the initial pain of parting it was surprising how swiftly he had faded out of her heart. If it had been love, real and true, she would still be longing for him, still suffering, wanting desperately to see him – instead of dreading it.

Clarrissa was barely up and about when a phone call came for her that made her eyes shine with a lustre that had been missing for a long time. "Oh, Lucy, Lucy," she breathed, the tips of her fingers pressed to her lips. "I've just made up my mind about something. I want you to go home, darling, I – well – I'm worried about Lorn and my sweet little Sherry. Go back and hold the fort for a while – just till I return in about a week."

"Oh stop it, Clarrissa," said Lucy quietly. "Worried about Lorn indeed! You're trying to get rid of me and damned fine you know it!"

The older girl laughed with delight. "I never could pull the wool over your eyes, could I? If you must know, that was Andrew on the phone. He's coming here to stay for a while and keep me amused. Oh, you've no idea how he cheers me up, Lucy, telling me about all the things he's been up to in London – the places he's been to that I used to go. He's taking a holiday and the sweet dear wants to spend it here, near me. . . ."

"And then?" Lucy's voice was taut.

"Who knows – or cares – one never knows with Andrew."

"Will he be coming back to Ardben with you?"

"Lucy! What on earth is the matter with you? I told you I don't know. Oh, be happy for me, do. Look, take the car and drive back today – go and enjoy a bit of freedom away

161

from me, you've been cooped up here for ages and never a word of complaint out of you."

Impulsively, she threw her arms round Lucy's neck and kissed her cheek. "Thank you, for being such a dear, patient little thing."

"But my place is here with you – I shouldn't go," protested Lucy, even while her heart raced with joy at the thought of going back to Moorgate House.

"Don't be such a stuffy little matron!" scolded Clarrissa happily. "I'm loads better, go this minute and get your things together – oh – look at me! I'm such a mess, I must go and do my face. Give Sherry a big hug from me and tell Lorn he needn't come on Sunday, I might be out with Andrew."

Half an hour later Lucy was bowling along the road, her mind speeding quicker than the wheels of the car which wasn't taking her back fast enough – back to Kintyre and Lorn.

His delight at seeing her was overwhelming. He had just finished evening surgery and was coming out of the door at the top of the hall.

She was standing in the hall doorway, silhouetted against the light. He looked up and saw her and she could almost feel the quickening of his heart, the tensing of his body.

He came forward slowly and before he reached her she said in a breathless whisper, "I'm alone, Lorn. Andrew phoned, he's spending a few days near Clarrissa; thought it would be nice to take her out and about. I wasn't needed so I – came home – I didn't even think to phone you."

His steps quickened, then he was beside her, looking down at her, drinking in her fragile beauty, his eyes black with joy, disbelief, desire. He held out his arms and she

162

went into them and it seemed the most natural thing in the world that his lips should be pressed against her hair, that he should be burying his face into the warmth of her neck. "My little Lucy," he murmured hoarsely. "It must be eternity since last I looked at your sweet dear face, heard your voice. I've been an empty shell without you. I went to the hospital – twice I went without catching so much as a glimpse of you."

"I know, I know," the tears were rolling down her cheeks, tears of happiness, washing the pain out of her heart. She raised her face to him and he kissed the tears away, his mouth so gentle it was like the touch of thistledown.

He drew back his head and for an abiding moment his amber-flecked eyes gazed deeply into hers before his lips sought hers, nuzzling and playing, deeper and deeper till the world spun round and encircled them in a warm, beating sphere that was theirs alone. They came back to reality after an eternity of wild, deep kisses that left them dazed and looking into each other's eyes with naked longing.

"Oh, my sweetheart, I've waited for this moment for so long," he whispered. "I can't believe it's real, now, here you are, in my arms, where I've imagined you in a million sleepless nights – a million dreams."

She laughed shakily. "I flew here on wings – not wheels; it seemed as if you were standing at every bend of the road, beckoning me. I said your name over and over, it was like poetry, it's always been like that since first I heard it. Lorn, Lorn, Lorn. I love it."

"Just my name?" he asked, all at once serious.

But she evaded the question by looking at her watch. "Heavens! I never realised, Meg must be here – in the kitchen . . ." Her voice had dropped to a horrified whisper.

"Darling, darling, don't worry," he reassured her. "She isn't here; she hasn't been for the last few days. Bob took a turn for the worse and she's had to stay with him constantly. He's getting over it now, though."

"Oh, poor Meg – but . . ." she stared at him. "How have you managed without her? What about meals?"

He smiled sheepishly. "I'm not exactly helpless you know. Meg left plenty of supplies. . . ."

"But you haven't bothered to cook, have you?" she accused, in angry concern.

"Bread and cheese: it's a grand standby . . ."

"Lorn! I'm going this very minute to the kitchen. Bread and cheese! And you a doctor who should know better about nutrition and the importance of proper meals!"

They laughed together, delighting in all the silly little things of the moment. A little whimper came from behind and Lucy turned to see Sherry in the kitchen doorway, his brown eyes full of reproach, one paw raised in abject appeal. She stooped to hug the little spaniel saying, "You too, starved to a shadow – well, not quite, you could do with being on a diet. Come on then, I'll feed you first."

A few minutes later Sherry's nose was buried in the bowl Lucy had set down for him, his golden brown body quivering with delight. She stood watching him eat then she glanced round the bright kitchen. It was going to be lovely, being here, just her and Lorn, cooking for him, tending to him. It was such a shame about Meg . . .

The thought suddenly struck her: no one knew she was here. The village had been quiet and deserted when she had driven through. The realisation made her tremble. Herself and Lorn, here alone in Moorgate House. It was

164

wonderful – yet – she quivered again, but would not allow her thoughts to stray further. Instead she went to the fridge to search out steak, eggs, bacon and a bottle of white wine, beautifully chilled, as if it had been waiting there for an occasion like this.

When Lorn came into the kitchen the savoury smell of grilling steak and bacon made him stop and sniff appreciatively. Lucy, with one of Meg's aprons tied round her middle, was at the stove, hot and slightly anxious looking, as she alternated her attention between the steaks under the grill and the eggs and tomatoes in the frying pan.

"I thought we would just have it here in the kitchen," she told him as she peered under the grill. "Oh I do hope these will be alright. Mother always said my nursing was more successful than my cooking—" She broke off abruptly; he had caught her round the waist and was kissing the nape of her neck. He smelled of soap and she knew he had just washed.

"I wouldn't notice if the steaks were burnt to a frazzle. I'm in too much of a ferment to care about anything else but you. I feel as if I'm dreaming and that I'll wake up in a minute and find you have gone from me."

"Lorn, the steaks!" she cried. "Go and sit down – this minute," she ordered. "You aren't dreaming and I'm doing my best to look after you by cooking you some sort of ghastly meal."

But it wasn't ghastly, it was delicious, yet even so they ate in a trance, each acutely aware of the other. He poured the wine and they sipped it, looking over the rims of the glasses into each other's eyes. A memory came unbidden to her, of eating and drinking in a hotel room with the brother of the man she sat with now. How different it had been: the meal had been lavish and expensive, the surroundings unnatural and the man . . .!

How different from his brother in every way imaginable. It was a beautiful experience to sit with him here, in the informality of the kitchen, eating steak and eggs and drinking wine.

He read her thoughts. "I think this is the most wonderful meal I've ever tasted and the company is perfect."

"I've hardly spoken a word," she laughed self-consciously.

"You don't have to; just to look at you is enough for me."

"Is it, Lorn?" she asked seriously.

He put his glass down and said with slow deliberation, "No, Lucy, it isn't – I want you with every fibre of my being – but I will respect your feelings in the matter. We're alone here in this house, just you and me . . . and no one knows that but the two of us."

He was voicing her earlier thoughts and she looked down at her plate, not meeting his eyes.

"Lucy," he went on softly, "why did we go to each other in the hall just now – without hesitation or doubt? It was as if we had both been waiting for such a moment. You made me make a promise to you – not to touch you, and I kept that promise, though it took me all my self-control to do so – yet, out there you came to me – as if you knew all along that it was going to happen – as if it was meant to happen."

"Yes, I know, Lorn – but – it doesn't make it right, does it?" Her voice was low, her mind a seething mass of contradictions.

"No," he said at last, "it doesn't make it right. We'll let things run in their natural course and meanwhile be

166

happy we are just here together, in our own little world of make believe . . . Now, young lady . . ." He stood up. "Get me an apron and I'll help with the dishes, even make-believe doesn't relieve us of all the tedious chores of domestic life."

But with laughter filling the kitchen the task of clearing up was a joy instead of a chore. She screamed with mirth at the sight of him in a plastic apron decorated with an enormous picture of a well-known brand of sauce and he laughed too because her happiness was so infectious.

Later, they walked hand in hand over the lawns to the little cove, with Sherry running at their heels. The sea hushed peacefully against the rocks, rattling the pebbles, tossing seaweed back and forth in the shallow water.

They stood together, her face on his shoulder, loving the feel of his rough tweed jacket, thrilled by his male nearness. His hand came round her waist to pull her in closer and they walked over the white sands to a group of rocks which were chiselled to fantastic shapes by wind and time.

She stood with her back against one and he stood tall in front of her, the palms of his hands against the craggy rock surface. Slowly he leaned over and kissed her lips, so softly she thought she had imagined it for her eyes were closed. She didn't want him to see what was in their depths.

"We have such a short time together." His lilting words twisted her heart. "But tomorrow is Friday, and after that the weekend is ours to do with as we will. . . . You might, of course, want to get away from the house – I can't keep you a prisoner . . ."

She knew what he meant. To have what they both wanted she mustn't be seen by anyone. As far as everyone knew she was still away with Clarrissa.

"A prisoner!" she cried, seeing him through a mist of tears. "Here with you – in this place? No, no, Lorn, it's the one thing I want more than anything in the world! I could stay here forever and never be weary." She laughed in confusion. "Meg has left so much in the freezer you would think she had abandoned you on a desert island."

"Your hands are cold." He took them and put them to his lips. "Let's go back – I'll play the piano for you if you would like."

"I didn't know you could play; I've never heard you."

"I used to – a lot, it was a form of relaxation for me. Och, I'm not very good, but I tell you what, I'll play and you sing. You can – beautifully. Don't forget, I heard you with the bairns that night in kirk."

But she didn't. Instead she sat back and listened to him, watched his long sensitive fingers drawing music from the piano, music that told of the wild beauty of the Highlands. In the enchantment of his playing he brought the sigh of the sea into the room; the chuckling of the hill burns; the wind keening over the moors; the simple haunting beauty of the primitive boat songs.

In her mind's eye she could see the fishing boats against the sunset and the men, triumphant after a good day's fishing, coming home to wives and sweethearts. It was like nothing she had ever heard before. It seemed as if all his emotions were flooding out through his fingers, releasing his torment, his loneliness . . . his love.

She shut her eyes and cried silently, wanting this magical night to last forever. Oh, Lorn, dearest Lorn, her heart wept, you have suffered so much, your sweet, gentle soul has been bruised and hurt beyond belief. I sit here and watch your dear face lost in rapture. At this moment you are happy, Lorn, and I want to make you happier. You deserve nothing else but happiness for the rest of your days.

The playing had stopped and he was above her, looking down at her. "Forgive me," she cried out in appeal to him. "Forgive me for crying – it was beautiful – if only this night could go on and on."

He took her hands and pulled her up to him. "We have a week of wonderful nights ahead of us, my darling – and if that is all I must have with you – then the memories will live with me forever."

But she pulled her hands out of his and went to the door. "Give me time, Lorn, give me tonight – to think."

"Goodnight, Lucy," he said quietly, and allowed her to go from the room without touching her again. She lay all night in a half-dreaming world of torment. She ached for him, she wanted to get up and run to his room and lie beside him, but something held her back, something for which there was no answer.

But there was, and she knew it. He was a married man, bound in a marriage that had no substance, but which yet wouldn't allow him to be free. He had told her he wanted her but that didn't mean that he loved her.

She tossed and turned in her suffering; her body burned for him – yet still she couldn't bring herself to get up and go to him – and she knew he wouldn't come to her. This wasn't Andrew – this was a man with principles.

At last she sank into a restless sleep, filled with dreams, filled with Lorn, and she awoke with a start to see the sun streaming down on the world outside. The hands of the clock were at nine. She had overslept and Lorn would be starting morning surgery without a decent breakfast inside him.

She reproached herself bitterly as she showered and

hastily pulled on a primrose yellow dress that matched her hair. She wandered down to the kitchen and fed a delighted Sherry, but she wasn't hungry enough to eat anything herself and sat at the table drinking coffee, lost in a reverie.

It was another glorious day of cloudless skies and she felt she had to get outside, to think, to decide. She went up the hall and out of the back door to the left of the surgery and walked over the dewy lawns. She looked back, thinking of Lorn tending his patients, but the surgery extension was hidden from her view by a thick screen of evergreens. And it was as well! She wasn't supposed to be here. To have had the folk of the village peering at her from the windows would have finished everything.

But it was finished anyway. She made the decision as she walked blindly over the rocks on the shore. She knew now what she had known all along and wouldn't admit to herself. She loved Lorn! She had loved him from the very first moment of their meeting. She had lied to herself about it, told herself she pitied him his miserable life with Clarrissa. But this swelling, growing, gnawing ache inside her very soul wasn't pity; it was love, pure and deep.

She loved him so much she felt she could live forever and never be able to show him how much she worshipped him – but she would never get the chance to show him how she felt about him for she knew she had to get away from him if she wanted to retain a shred of reason.

She couldn't think straight with him so close. Oh the irony of it! She had fled to this place to escape Andrew and had ended up falling in love with his married brother!

What she had felt for Andrew was a mere illusion compared to this love that enveloped her. She gave a short little laugh of misery as she tried to recall her feelings

170

after the break with Andrew. She had thought then that that was what the pain of a lost love was like. Compared to what she felt now it had been a tiny pin-prick, hurting for a time but soon forgotten.

She knew now why she had come back to Moorgate House with such eagerness after the New Year holiday; why she had borne Nora Bruce's jibes; how she had put up with Clarrissa's tempers. It was because she would have suffered anything just so long as she was beside the man she really loved, the man she had loved from the time she stepped into his car on a cold, bleak December dusk – such a long time ago it now seemed.

Stopping for a moment she gazed unseeingly out over the Atlantic. How could she tell him she was leaving? How could she rob him of the happiness she had glimpsed last night? Watch the bleak hurt filling his brown eyes till they were black and empty?

She looked at her watch. It was almost ten and he would be finishing surgery, eagerly hurrying into the house to look for her before he went off on his morning rounds.

She decided she would wait till he had gone then she would go back and pack some things. Hugh the postman would be coming back from his rounds about eleven. If she waited on him he would give her a lift into Tarbert and then . . .

She planned no further, she only knew she had to get away from here before it was too late. She sat down on a rock and let ten minutes elapse; minutes in which she saw the future stretching before her, as black and as empty as space. Then she stood up and began to hurry back the way she had come, panic in her now lest she wouldn't have time to pack and be away before Lorn's return.

She was crying, the tears pouring unchecked down her

face. The world was a misty blur and she saw not where she was going. Her foot caught and twisted on a slimy rock and she put out a hand to save herself. But it was too late; she felt herself falling, heard a dull thud inside her head.

For a few seconds she lay looking up at the sky – or was it the sea? Wavering and rolling, surging on top of her in a dizzy whirl that drowned her senses, and everything went black.

Deep down in the depths of her subconscious she was aware of strong arms lifting her, carrying her on and on, ever and ever upwards towards the empty spaces in the sky, but no matter how high she was carried she was sinking lower and lower, down, down . . .

She gave a little moan of terror and put out a hand to clutch at something, anything that would lift her up out of the depths of darkness . . .

And a gentle hand reached out and took hers, holding it reassuringly, making her feel secure and unafraid. . . .

Now she was floating on a cloud that supported her body so that she was no longer sinking but instead was safe and warm. Another cloud wept rain on her forehead and it was cool and soothing, so relaxing that she let her own special cloud drift her peacefully and gently through velvet reaches to a dreamland that allowed her mind and body to sink into deep and healing oblivion.

Chapter Eighteen

Slowly she floated out of deep dark night towards daylight. She opened her eyes and focused them on an oak-beamed ceiling that was familiar to her. Her gaze travelled downwards to the walls, white walls, sprinkled with rosebuds.

A tear of relief slid over her cheeks. She was in her bedroom in Moorgate House, the room she felt safe in, her own little haven with its homely peaceful atmosphere and simple furnishings.

The curtains were drawn across the window but it was very bright outside and she knew that the sun was shining and the birds were singing. How long had she been lying here? she asked herself. She knew it wasn't all that early – the sun was too high in the sky for that – so why was she here in bed when she should be up seeing to things . . .?

The memory of her walk over the shore came back to her with a jolt – that, and her decision to pack her bags and leave Lorn.

She lifted her head in mild panic. Her yellow dress lay neatly over the back of a chair; the dress she had put on that morning before leaving the house. But was it still the same morning – the same day even? She felt as if she had been asleep for hours. . . .

Footsteps sounded on the stairs and came up the corridor. The door opened and Lorn stood there, his eyes lighting with relief at seeing her awake. He came forward, his mouth relaxing into a smile. "You've decided to come back to me," he said softly, and she wondered dazedly if he had known that she was going to leave him. "You've been out for two hours. . . ."

Relief forced her head back into the pillows. She had misconstrued his meaning. He didn't know what she had been planning to do; how could he? "Two hours? You mean – it's still the same day?"

He chuckled, and sitting down on the bed took her hands. "Yes, my darling, you gave your head a nasty bump on the rocks. I couldn't find you in the house and thought you would be down on the shore so I came to look for you. When I saw you lying there – I thought – oh, my dear little Lucy . . ."

For a moment he couldn't go on, and she raised her hand to gently touch the lock of hair on his forehead. "I'm a silly fool, falling like that, but – how did I get here?"

"I carried you of course; you aren't heavy. You gave your head quite a bump on the rocks and knocked yourself out. No bones broken or anything, so I just put you to bed, bathed your brow and then let you sleep. How are you – any headache?"

"Just a slight muzziness . . ." Her eyes strayed once more to the dress lying over the chair. "Did you . . .?"

"Stop blushing," he teased her. "I only took off your dress and shoes to make you more comfortable. Where's your nightdress and you can slip it on?"

"Over there, in that silly octopus pyjama case." She smiled. "Mother made it for my fourteenth birthday and I have never parted with it. But," she struggled

174

to sit up, "I must get up, there's nothing wrong with me."

"You're staying where you are for another hour or two – doctor's orders; it's my turn to nurse you for a bit. I'm going to bring you up something to eat. . . ."

He had pulled her nightdress out of the case and it was his turn to blush as he looked at the flimsy scrap of black silky fabric dangling from his fingers. "Will you be warm enough with this on?" he asked doubtfully and she gave a burst of laughter.

"Dear, dear, Lorn, girls don't wear things like that to be warm; it's the feel of the material that's good and the luxury of knowing that you look glamorous – even if you're the only one to know it. Lorn! You're blushing like a schoolboy – oh give it to me – and I'd love that bite to eat you promised."

He was back in a short time with tea, toast and scrambled eggs. In a glass tumbler was a rather ungainly posy of narcissus and tulips, the sight of which brought a rush of love to her heart. "Oh Lorn," she whispered, "it's the nicest bouquet anyone has ever given me."

He shuffled and looked embarrassed once more. "I'm not very good at things like that."

She took his hands and kissed the back of each one tenderly. "Pretty bows don't always bind the nicest packages. It's the thought that counts more than anything. Thank you, Lorn – and also for making me my lunch."

"I've got to go out for a while." He was at the door, the awkwardness still on him. "You eat everything on that tray now – with the exception of the flowers, of course! Afterwards you can laze about and do whatever you like – till I come back. . . . By the way . . ." he grinned, "you look beautiful lying there in that black handkerchief thing!"

175

The door shut and she lay back on the pillows feeling warm and contented. All her earlier urges to run away had left her. She ate hungrily then sat back, letting the peace of the silent house wash over her. Her eyes closed and she felt herself drifting back into sleep. Her dreams no longer tormented her but were full of wonderful images. Lorn was enmeshed into all of them and she was gliding towards him, her nightdress blowing gently in a hush of a breeze that ruffled her hair. She was reaching out to him and he was coming to her, running but in slow motion. He was naked and the sun had turned his body to gold. She could see his muscles rippling, a pulse beating swiftly in his neck, his arms reaching out to her . . .

"Lorn, Lorn," she murmured. 'Stay with me, please stay."

"I'm here, Lucy."

She opened her eyes to see him by her bed. He could have been standing there for minutes or hours, she didn't know. She felt relaxed and warm. "Lorn, you're back, what time is it?"

"Four o'clock, you lazy wee thing." His voice was low. "How do you feel now?"

"Wonderful." She stretched her arms above her head then drew them down quickly, knowing that he could see her breasts through the flimsy nightdress. She opened her eyes wide to look at his face, noting the thin little hollows in his cheeks, the deep cleft of the dimple in his strong chin. Somewhere deep down in her belly a nerve quivered, the beat of it growing stronger till it throbbed through her entire body. She loved him, oh how she loved him, and she wasn't going to deny him any longer. He had been so patient with her, so very patient.

"Lorn." She put up her hand and pulled his dark head

176

down towards her, her fingers curling into the hollow at the nape of his neck. Tenderly she kissed the dimple on his chin and stroked the unruly lock of hair from his brow. Her eyes looked deep into his and she breathed, "I love you, Lorn."

"Lucy." His lips melted against hers, warm, firm, passionate lips that clung and played with hers. With a soft little moan she responded to him wildly, her body tingling with pleasure as his hands caressed her, awakening her to raptures she had never experienced with any other man.

Deeper and deeper they kissed, their mouths were mobile instruments of pleasure, taking, giving. His tongue was warm, probing, playing with hers, exploring all the soft, moist niches of her mouth. He lifted her head and cradled it in his hands, playing with the curls, kissing them, nuzzling her ears, sending shivers of delight and aching longing through the very marrow of her body.

Through a haze of tears she saw his beloved face, the finely-honed features, the firm sensual mouth, so near, ready to take hers again – and again . . . and again . . .

A little dew of perspiration lay on his forehead and she put up a tender finger to stroke it away. With a little laugh he caught her fingers in his teeth and ran his lips over her fingertips, slowly, slowly, the dark eyes that held hers burning with longing.

She raised both her arms and stroked his neck then her hands slid to the front of his shirt. She unbuttoned it and it slid off his shoulders. His body was lean and firm, the skin soft, cool at the first brief touch before the heat of it burned into her hands.

In a daze she felt him removing the flimsy veil of her nightdress. She lay passively as his gaze travelled over the pale beauty of her body to the milky whiteness of her breasts.

"Lucy, oh Lucy, you're so beautiful," he said huskily, tremblingly. His dark head came down, his mouth played sensually with her nipples. She gave a cry, everything in her erupting into pure and naked yearning. She wanted to be loved by him as she had never wanted it with any other; she wanted him to take her, to own her . . .

She stiffened suddenly. Through all the welter of desire and longing that throbbed in her body a thought burst into her brain and wouldn't go away. She could never belong to him; he belonged to another! It was wrong, wrong, to lie in this bed, in this house, allowing herself to be loved by another woman's husband!

She pressed her hand to her mouth but couldn't stop the agonised cry that tore from her. "No, Lorn, no! It's wrong! Wrong!"

He drew away from her to stare at her in disbelief. She turned her head on the pillow but he caught her chin in his hand and forced her to look at him. "Lucy, for God's sake," he said softly. "Don't do this to me."

She shook her head from side to side in her torment. "I'm sorry, oh, my darling, I'm sorry but I can't – I can't . . ."

"A fine time to tell me!" he exploded harshly. "What the hell do you think I am? A wax dummy? I'm flesh and blood, Lucy! I may be wrong but I had the silliest notion a few moments ago that you were made of the same stuff!"

His jaw was tight with anger and he scrambled away from her to pull his shirt roughly over his shoulders. Without doing up the buttons he sat on the edge of the bed punching his clenched fists together, then he brought

178

them up to tap the thumbnails against his teeth, his eyes staring broodingly ahead, seeing nothing.

"Oh, Lorn, I don't want to hurt you," her voice broke on a sob. "It would be different if Clarrissa didn't depend on you so much – if – if she was even leaving you as she keeps threatening. . . ."

"She *is* leaving me!" His voice was hard with pent up emotions. "She told me before she went away to the nursing home that it was only a matter of time before she left me for good – oh, not yet . . ." He laughed mirthlessly. "She hasn't quite finished with me, she'll play cat and mouse for a while longer before she finally waves goodbye."

Lucy felt herself drowning with her love for him. Slowly she reached out to him and laid her hand on his arm. Savagely he caught it and raised it to his lips to kiss it.

"I love you, Lucy," he said, his voice so choked with emotion she could barely hear it. "I loved you from the first moment I saw you standing in the hall looking like a lost child. Your hair was damp with tiny curls clinging round your ears and your eyes were big with uncertainty – yet there was spirit in them too – you had the look of a girl who had been recently hurt but who was determined to battle on and pick up the pieces of her life."

He gazed down at his hands. "I want to give you everything – at the moment I can only give you my love – later – oh, quite a bit later, when Clarrissa makes up her mind to finally leave – I will ask you to be my wife – if you think you can wait that long."

She laughed shakily. "My darling, I wish I could say honestly that I would wait forever if need be – but there would be no point in lying. I can't wait forever – perhaps

179

a year – or two – but right now . . ." She pulled his head down towards her, "We neither of us are going to wait a moment longer – for this . . ."

Now there was no holding back for either of them. They whirled together towards dizzy heights of rapture, lost, lost in sweet, delirious ecstasy, captured in a world in which there was no time, aware only of each other, of swiftly-beating hearts, of their bodies meeting and merging, searching, exploring the wonders of human sensuality, reaching ever further for one another till it seemed their very souls soared heavenwards.

Afterwards they lay together, warm and sleepy, his head on her breasts while she stroked his dark curling hair. "Now I know what true love is really like," she whispered. "All these months I pretended to myself that what I felt for you was the kind of feeling any woman would have for a man putting up with the things you do. I kept on deceiving myself – but this morning I couldn't pretend any longer. I had to admit to myself I loved you . . . and I was going to leave you, for I knew it was wrong to want another woman's husband. Then I fell – you found me and I have let you make love to me, but somehow I don't feel it was wrong. Can love be wrong, Lorn?"

"No, darling, but the circumstances of it can't always be right." In the warm circle of his arms, her head now against his broad deep chest, hearing the thudding of his beloved heart, she felt safe and protected, even though sadness washed over her at his words.

Clarrissa would come back; she wouldn't leave till it suited her. There was no knowing what went on in her mind from one minute to the next – but – Lucy snuggled closer to Lorn – no matter how little time she had to spend with him she resolved it would be the most precious

180

experience of their lives; an interlude that they could later look back on and remember only gladness.

He kissed the tip of her nose and broke reluctantly away from her embrace. "I'm going to have a shower before I take evening surgery. You lie there and have a rest – after all—" he grinned, "you've had a very trying and exhausting day."

She giggled and threw a cushion at him and lay, feeling deliciously relaxed, till she heard him emerging from the bathroom, then she got up, wrapped herself in her robe, and went to run a bath for herself, pouring in generous amounts of bubble bath and two scented capsules of bath oil. In this perfumed mixture she soaked for fully twenty minutes before getting dressed and running down to the kitchen to start preparing a meal.

She was breaking the normal routine of the house and she was glad. It meant a longer evening for them both. She knew he disliked the formality of the late dinner with Clarrissa and her mother dressing up, going through all the motions of a way of life that wasn't in keeping with country ways.

Sherry sat with his nose in his paws, watching her as she went about humming a little tune of joy. She felt none the worse for her fall of the morning and she stopped in the act of stirring a pan of gravy.

So much had happened since her walk over the shore that she was astonished to think it was still the same day. She felt contented and fulfilled beyond measure. She and Lorn had loved, and in doing so had stepped over a threshold from which there was no return. For months now he had owned her heart – now he owned her body. It was a revelation that was almost spiritual and

181

she stood for a long time, the spoon suspended over the pan, lost in deep reflection.

Sherry whined, watching her intently, his stumpy tail beating the floor and she giggled and stooped to hug him. "Alright, I know what you want. Sit still now and I'll get you some dinner."

The door at the top of the hall closed softly and she stiffened, listening to the approaching footsteps, no longer wearily slow but firm and sure. He came into the kitchen, his face alight. "That's it, darling, barring emergencies I'm a free man for two whole days. Oh, Lucy, we're going to make the most of every second. Come here, I've missed you."

"But I saw you just over an hour ago," she protested with a smile, but she went into his arms willingly.

"Let's pretend," he murmured into her hair, "that we're on our honeymoon and that you're my young and very new bride."

"Alright," she agreed happily. "And new brides aren't supposed to be able to cook so it will be apt in that sense anyway."

"In every sense, my sweet, dear love." His eyes burned into hers, filled once more with dark desire.

Chapter Nineteen

After dinner they walked hand in hand through the gardens, silent, enraptured with the perfect evening. The scent of peat smoke drifted from a distant crofthouse; the gulls wheeled lazily on the buoyant air thermals above; Sherry was a golden shadow against a golden horizon that met a sea washed with silver and sprinkled with the colours of opals.

Dusk came down, as gentle as a baby's breath, and in the slight chill of a purpled gloaming he slid his arm round her waist to draw her into the warmth of his body. They went back to the house and he set a match to the fire and soon the logs were hissing in the flames, glowing over the room, touching the furthest corners with a warm hue.

He reached over and kissed her on the brow and said almost apologetically, "I must phone the hospital, sweetheart. Clarrissa will wonder if I don't. . . ."

She put a finger over his lips. "Hush, darling, I understand, I'm going upstairs anyway, to change."

She came back wearing silk pyjamas in a soft blue, and the firelight gilded her creamy skin. "How is Clarrissa?" she asked him, a sense of guilt in her as she spoke the name.

He looked thoughtful. "She's . . . well, to be truthful, she's cheerful – Andrew must be good for her. She thinks she'll be away for a few more days. . . ."

All the while he was speaking he couldn't take his eyes off Lucy and he said no more. They went into each other's arms without words. They kissed and sank to the rug in front of the fire. They were both awash with a passion that knew no bounds. She wore nothing under the pyjamas and he drew them from her body, covering her with kisses that left her gasping.

For a moment she wondered if he thought her shameless coming to him like this but he swept away her doubts in a tide of untamed desire. The rug was warm and soft beneath them, the firelight poured over their naked bodies. This time he couldn't hold himself back, forgot to be gentle, but she didn't care; she was beyond caring about anything because she was drowning in the waves of heat that coursed through her, goading him to an abandonment that made him go wild.

They moved together as one; one flesh; one spirit; one pulsing throbbing heart; one fire that totally consumed them, nothing, no one existed outside themselves. Their mouths met over and over, instruments of pleasure that magnified the other pleasures they were sharing. Their cries came together, mingling and meeting without restraint. Then he was kissing her again and again, pledging his love to her, holding her close, not moving away from her and for a little while they slept like that, locked together as if they were unwilling to become separate entities again.

Afterwards they sat, arms entwined, gazing into the fire, Sherry snoring softly; the clock ticking; logs crackling and spitting in the hearth, but otherwise nothing else stirred.

For a long time they cuddled close together, saying little, then he got up and padded through to the kitchen to make cocoa, bringing it to her with a plate of biscuits.

184

"I can't remember when I was last so happy," he told her as they sipped the steaming mugfuls. "It must have been in another world."

She put her pinky into the dimple in his chin and smiled then she turned from him, her knees drawn to her chin, and said, "You must have been happy once, Lorn, you and Clarrissa – I'm sorry, darling, but you should talk about it. She's very beautiful, you and she . . ."

"I was enchanted with her – yes – I'd be lying if I said otherwise. She swept me off my feet, I couldn't think straight . . . and that's why it was all wrong. It was all too quick . . . I wanted her so badly I mistook physical attraction for love. I was infatuated with her but after the initial fires died down I soon realised we had nothing in common.

"Clarrissa is a butterfly; gaudy, extravagant, restlessly flitting from one bright flower to the next and never quite finding satisfaction in anything. She's an extrovert while I . . . I like my own space, to be at one with the world. Perhaps that's where I went wrong with her: for the sake of peace I gave in to her every whim, let her have her own way till she got out of hand and I didn't know how to deal with her.

"Oh, we hobbled along – for two and a half years, never quite meeting but never quite parting either . . . then – the baby came . . . You know the rest. She blames me bitterly for what happened and I look at her and remember how she used to be and I feel guilty. I can't fight back. I should, I know, but the roof would cave in on me if I did; Clarrissa and her mother – on and on at me – without end.

"It's bad enough the way it is – I can't take the risk of making it worse. There's another thing: I can't completely forget how it once was. I don't love her now, I know I

185

never did – but I can't dislike her either, no matter what she says or does to me – I feel so sorry she's the way she is, and in a way I understand how she feels about me."

Lucy closed her eyes and a sob broke in her throat. Abruptly she turned to him and blindly sought the comfort of his arms. "Oh my poor darling, my Lorn," she choked. "I love you so much and even more for what you stand for. You could never hate anyone, it isn't in you and I know what you mean about her. She can be utterly mean one minute and the next, when she smiles, you forget all the nasty things and can't help liking her. I don't blame you one bit for falling under her spell."

He cupped her chin in his hand and made her face him. "Marry in haste, repent at leisure, that's what they say, isn't it? Yet if I could marry you tomorrow I know I would never regret it."

"Oh, Lorn, Lorn!" she cried, angry without knowing why. "Don't say such things. You don't even know me."

"Know you? I've known you all my life – waited for you all my life – you've been my life for more than five months now – yet – you're right, Lucy, I don't know much about you beyond the fact you're a Yorkshire lass, an excellent nurse – and you came here to get away from someone who broke your heart . . . I know now that the someone was my brother. That fact alone tears me in two. Andrew always got what he wanted. I hate the idea of you and him together – even though it's over."

"Please, Lorn, don't. It's all in the past; you're what matters now. I was infatuated with him, as you were with Clarrissa – but I can't really talk about it – not yet – I want only to think of us."

Tears glinted in her eyes and she turned sharply to look into the fire. She really couldn't expand on the subject of

Andrew; the wound was healing but it still hurt her to think of how he had cheated and lied to her, and she went on softly, "I told you just now you ought to talk about your feelings, yet, cheat that I am, I can't bring myself to talk about mine."

"I've had more time than you to think it all out," he told her tenderly. "You will talk – when you're ready."

That night they slept together in her room, safe and snug in the circle of each other's arms. He held her so close it was as if he was afraid she would somehow escape and not be there in the morning.

She woke first and lay for a long time looking at him in repose. His face was close to hers on the pillow and she could see the pulse of his life beating in his neck. He looked relaxed, so unlike the tense man who often drove himself to the point of exhaustion.

Was it to forget, she wondered, to forget how meaningless his life had become? Well, this was the weekend, *their* weekend, and she would make it as happy as she knew how. Love for him was brimming out of her heart. She wanted to give him everything; joy; peace; comfort, to cram a lifetime of happiness into the few days that were theirs.

His arms were locked so tightly round her she had to ease herself out of them bit by bit. He stirred and sighed and she froze, holding her breath, but he was soon peaceful again and she slipped her arms into her robe and went down to the kitchen.

Sherry rose from his basket to greet her, his stumpy tail a-wag with pleasure, and she gave him some milk to lap up then let him out. She stood for a minute by the open door, drinking in the sweet smell of dew-wet grass.

187

It was a hazy morning, calm and slightly frosty, but by the time the smell of sizzling bacon was filling the kitchen the banks of mist were rolling away and bright patches of blue showed in the pearly sky.

When she carried the tray upstairs he was stretching himself awake and when he saw her he sat up to look at her as if she wasn't real.

She put the tray down by the bedside. "Hey, what's this?" he smiled. "It looks and smells like real food! You're spoiling me, little Lucy, I can't remember when last I had breakfast in bed."

He held out his arms and she went into them. "I thought for a moment I was dreaming when I saw you just now," he breathed happily. "But never in my dreams did I imagine you would look as good as you do now with your golden curls rumpled and your face smooth and flushed from slaving over a hot stove. I think I would like to look at you forever."

"Later," she laughed. "I didn't make you breakfast for it to get cold while you study my face. Oh, Lorn, it's going to be a beautiful day. The sun's breaking through the mist. It's one of those days that will get warmer and warmer."

"We could go for a swim," he suggested eagerly as she poured tea. "Come on, I dare you." He laughed at the expression on her face. "You're a spoilsport, Lucy Pemberton – afraid of the water – just because it might be a bit cold."

But as the day progressed it became so warm she went eagerly to change into her swimsuit. Laughing, he took her hand and they sped over to the water that was gently lapping the white sands. Tentatively she dipped a toe into the shallows but he caught her up in his arms and carried her out to a rock pool. There he let her down none too gently and the shock of the cold water on her bare flesh made her shriek and cling to him.

He was having none of that, however. With a devilish chuckle he began splashing her unmercifully.

"Lorn! You beast!" she gasped. "I'll pay you back for that. . . ."

But he gave her no chance to retaliate, he had ducked down into the waves and was swimming about, shouting at her to stop being a baby and to come in beside him.

She held her breath and went in. The cold of the water took her breath away but after a few moments she grew used to it and soon she was swimming beside him, a delighted Sherry dog-paddling alongside, revelling in his new-found freedom. His mistress hated it if he so much as got his feet wet because it meant she couldn't nurse him on her knee. Now he barked joyfully, leaping at the oncoming waves, half swimming, half jumping over them, his tongue lolling out of the corner of his mouth.

The sun beat down warmly. It was a perfect day with a languorous feel to it, tiny puffs of cloud sailed serenely overhead; oystercatchers muttered among the rocks; eider ducks crooned; gannets plunged the waves; seals sunbathed on the reefs – and far in the shaded woodlands a cuckoo was calling, triumphantly, joyously.

Lucy swam to a rock and pulled herself up on it. "Listen!" she cried. "The cuckoo! Summer is really here now. I never think it's truly summer till I hear the cuckoo."

He caught her and kissed her, his fingers stroking the wet curls from her forehead. "Little cuckoo yourself," he said tenderly. "All daft and eager and happy." He put his arms around her. "I don't need the summer to bring the sun into my life with you here beside me; it's in your hair, those wonderful eyes of yours, that dear soft mouth I want to kiss and kiss. Your eyes are as blue as the sea today, my sweet, sweet summer child. I feel so aware of the world – as if it was all new to me, as if I was discovering the flowers, the trees – the cuckoo, for the first time!"

Putting his cheek next to hers he whispered, "And why is it I am aching again to make love to you? I can't get enough of you my darling. Today I am discovering the world again. Now I want to know what every part of your body looks like – to look – and to remember."

He took her hand and led her over the rocks, to lie together on the sand, hot beneath their bodies. The sun beat warmly over their naked flesh. They kissed and touched, lost in their passion for one another; united in a love that joined them together till their cries soared and mingled with those of the gulls in the skies above and then they fell asleep like contented children while the breeze played with their hair and the sun bronzed their bodies.

The next day, Lorn suggested that they go out in the boat. "Mind you," he laughed, running his hands over the keel, "I don't know if she's completely watertight. I haven't had a minute to get her ready for the water, but she ought to keep us afloat. We'll just dabble about in the bay."

Lucy met his suggestion with a clap of delight. "Oh, could we go fishing, please? Father took me out when we all used to go to the seaside for our holidays. He was the expert but I always caught the biggest fish and he said I was lucky with a rod."

He looked rueful. "Darling, I'm sorry. I snapped my rod on the rocks last year and never got round to getting another. I was going to see old Angus about—"

190

"Lorn, I nearly forgot!" she exclaimed. She looked like an excited small girl with her eyes sparkling in her tanned face. She was wearing the primrose dress that matched her sunbleached hair, her shapely limbs were golden brown and his gaze swept over her with admiration.

"What is it, you daft little cuckoo?" he said with a grin.

"Wait here." She pushed him down onto a sun-warmed rock. "Now, count to ten then shut your eyes and don't dare open them again till I say so."

Breathlessly she ran over the lawn into the house and up to her room. At the back of the cupboard was her Christmas present to Lorn and she grabbed it and fled back outside to the rock where he sat, his eyes exaggeratedly tight shut, a smile lurking at the corners of his mouth.

"I feel an idiot, sitting here like this," he laughed, as he heard her approach.

She went up to him and put her arms round his neck to kiss him warmly on the lips and to push the ungainly package into his hands. "Merry Christmas!" she cried. "You can open your eyes now."

He stared at the gaily-wrapped package and a flush crept over his face. Slowly he peeled off the wrappings and stared down at the fine new fishing rod. "Lucy, oh my Lucy," he murmured huskily. "What did I do to your kind little heart that day? I chased you out of the kitchen with my harsh words. I wanted to take the gift from you so that I could have an excuse to kiss you but instead I behaved like a boor. I was jealous – I kept seeing you in Andrew's arms; I wanted you for my own – and instead there you were with him. He always got what he wanted – took what he wanted – and very often he took it from me. When we were bairns he used to take my toys, when we grew older

191

he took more and more . . ." He gave a mirthless laugh. "Very often he took my girls, and I thought . . ."

The tears glinted in her eyes and she put a finger over his lips. "Hush, hush, my dearest. When you saw me with your brother you were seeing a girl in the arms of a man she had left England to escape. When he came here and saw me he got the idea that he could carry on where he had left off.

"I was torn in two and terribly confused. I thought I was still in love with him but it all came to a head when I went home with him at the New Year. I realised then that it was definitely over between us. I never dreamed what true love was until I came here – to Moorgate House – and you.

"Andrew was unreal from the start, I was dazzled by him, by his glamour and glitter. In a way I feel sorry for him now – life to Andrew is a plaything, he will never have what you and I have, my own dearest Lorn – he will never know – true love."

"Lucy," he cried and pulled her to his heart, his kisses savage in his relief at hearing her words. "Oh, it's so good to hold you like this – thank you for your love – and for this marvellous present. Come on, let's try it out." Grabbing her hand he ran with her along the shore and when they had gathered enough bait they hauled the boat into the water.

Sherry, determined not to be left out, jumped in beside them, and they bobbed about in the calm waters of the bay where the sea was green and deep and so clear it was possible to see right down to the sandy bottom.

They caught nothing but a crab and a barnacle-encrusted lower set of false teeth. When Lucy wound in the line and they saw the teeth dangling on the hook they clutched one another and shrieked aloud with uncontrollable mirth, made all the merrier when Sherry started barking as if he was sharing in the joke.

Lucy had carefully deposited her find on the thwart beside her and Lorn wiped his eyes and gasped. "I swear they belong to old Angus MacDonald. I mind him telling everyone he lost his teeth last summer when he was out fishing. He got so excited at seeing a shoal of herring he opened his mouth so wide his teeth fell out and though he caught as many silver darlings as his boat would hold he couldn't eat a single one without his teeth. It was liquids for him till he could get to see a dentist. Wait till I show him what we caught!"

They were still chuckling as they made their way back to the house and were in the kitchen deciding what to have for a meal when the phone shrilled from the sitting room. They both froze, looking at each other wordlessly. It was the first time the phone had rung all weekend. It could have been anybody but instinctively, they knew in those moments that their time together was almost over.

Taking a deep breath, Lorn strode into the sitting room to stare down at the shiny white instrument before snatching it up, while Lucy stood in the doorway watching, her heart suddenly cold and heavy in her breast.

"Darling," Clarrissa's voice crackled over the line. "I'm being allowed to go free! We'll be home tomorrow! No, Lorn, don't send Lucy, Andrew's bringing us – he'll be staying with us for a few days . . . Lorn, are you still there?"

"Yes, Clarrissa, I'm here."

"I've had the most marvellous time and I'm loads better! I've had all my tests and now all I have to do is wait for the results. Isn't this weather glorious?

I hope you and Lucy are behaving. Give her my love – oh and my poor darling Sherry! He must have missed me so – hug him for me. We'll be home around teatime. Bye for now."

Carefully Lorn replaced the receiver. Clarrissa's words rang in his ears. *I hope you and Lucy are behaving.* She knew! Of course she knew. She had sent Lucy back, had known they would be together in the house. She knew – and she didn't care. She would never have cared if he'd had one affair after another; that was the sum total of her feelings for him.

Perhaps – the thought struck him – she had wanted him to yield to temptation to add more fuel to her fires – to add to that which she already had over him. Could he go on with it? The accusations – the guilt . . . And now . . .

He put a hand up to his eyes and Lucy gave a little cry and ran to him. "Darling, don't, please don't!"

"It's over, Lucy," he said brokenly. "I had hoped for a few more days – but it's over."

"Not yet, we still have one more night," she whispered, though she felt like crying out in her deepest agony of heartache.

He was stroking her hair, his hand trembling. "Clarrissa knows about us, Lucy," he said in a low voice.

"I know," she murmured. "I've already thought about it – and wondered – have we fallen into a trap? Oh, Lorn, I'm afraid, afraid because I want to spend the rest of my life near you, yet not knowing if I'm strong enough to stand up to Clarrissa and her mother – especially her mother. I can handle Clarrissa – but – it might be better for everyone if I was to go away after all."

"No! No, Lucy!" The cry was torn from him. "Don't leave me to face it alone! Darling, I love you." He cupped

194

her chin in his hands and she looked up to see the tears shimmering on his thick lashes and his throat working with emotion.

"Lucy," he went on, "in the last three days I have never, never been so happy. You have given me pleasure and joy beyond belief. I have laughed such as I have never laughed in my life before – and—" his voice broke, "I have cried as I am crying now for the love of a pure and beautiful girl who has my heart in her keeping. Don't leave me, my darling. Please don't make me say goodbye again."

She nuzzled her face against his cheek and held him as if she would never let go of him. "I won't leave you, Lorn," she said softly, even while she knew they couldn't go on with their love in the same house together, pretending, stealing moments of love, all the time watching to see if they were being watched, alert, wary, nervous.

The thought was unbearable and she pushed it away. Tonight was still theirs and she lifted her face for his kiss. That night they clung to each other passionately but even as they made love there was an ache inside each of them and a terrible uncertainty for the days that lay ahead.

Chapter Twenty

They arrived the next day at four, Clarrissa laughing and happy, Nora Bruce fussing, bemoaning the fact that Meg wasn't there at Moorgate House to see to things, Andrew as cocksure and as handsome as ever, eyeing Lucy covertly, taunting her with his smile.

The peace of the house was invaded, loud voices shrilled in the rooms. Lorn's gaze caught Lucy's and there was despair and sadness in the look.

"Oh I'm so utterly exhausted!" Clarrissa's voice rang out. "I simply must go and lie down for a while. Come, Sherry, up! Oh my angel, I've missed you so."

There were no such loving exclamations over Lorn. Instead she gave him a sidelong glance and said thoughtfully, "You do look different, Lorn, dear – contented – yes, I think that's the word for you."

Andrew laughed and gave Lucy a conspiratorial wink. "What did you expect, Rissa, darling? If I had a sweet little nurse like Lucy to look after my every need I think I too would be very contented."

It was starting, already it was starting, and Lucy knew her surmise had been correct. She and Lorn had fallen into a trap, a web, and with every minute that passed they were becoming more and more entangled.

Andrew kept up the innuendoes all evening, ably aided

by Clarrissa, until Lucy felt she could take no more.

When the opportunity arose she caught hold of Andrew in the hall and hissed at him furiously, "Will you stop it! Please, stop it!"

He looked at her in affected surprise. "Stop what, my lovely? You're imagining things. You, of all people, should know I would never do anything to hurt you."

He put his arm round her waist with familiar intimacy, and tried to kiss her, but she struggled away from him. "How dare you? Who do you think you are? You don't own me!"

He smiled carelessly. "No, I never quite managed that, did I Lucy? But . . ." he put his face close to hers and whispered jeeringly, "I bet big brother did! For all his quiet-spoken ways I bet he hit the jackpot alright; took what was mine. Oh, I knew you were soft on him – all those schoolgirl blushes whenever he appeared – his little sulks when—" She slapped his face, hard, and he put his hand up to it, his eyes glittering coldly in a face that was white with rage. "Little bitch! I'll tell you something; it was me who inveigled Rissa into letting you come back here." He laughed harshly. "I let her think I wanted to have her all to myself and the silly brat fell for it. You see, Lucy, I wanted to pay you back for rejecting me – the first girl ever to do so. I sent you running back here like a little rabbit – straight into the arms of a sex-starved man. But I'll see you pay for all the stolen thrills you took from a married man. You see if I don't."

The atmosphere in the house became intolerable. On the surface it appeared as normal as it ever would, with Clarrissa behaving in an oddly abandoned manner. She was highly excited, a wildness in her that

197

was somehow disquieting. Every evening she played the piano, extracting tunes that were stirring yet stifling.

Later, Andrew would put records on the stereo and he would sweep her up in his arms to whirl her round and round, both of them screeching with laughter as zingy dance music pounded through the room. When they weren't laughing they were being witty, the life and soul of the party, but at other times they taunted and teased both Lucy and Lorn.

Mealtimes were occasions to be dreaded; they were at their worst then, always implying that they were sharing some secret joke, something that only they knew about.

Lorn became white and strained again; the Lorn that he had been before. Gone was all the happiness he and Lucy had shared for a few brief, wonderful days.

Lucy lay in bed at night unable to sleep, hearing him in his room, so near, yet so far. She also heard Andrew, fumbling around, bumping into things because very often he had taken too much to drink, and silently, with the tears running down her cheeks, she prayed that he would be gone soon.

But he had taken two weeks' leave – and there was still more than a week of it to go. She got no chance to be alone with Lorn, to tell him how much she loved him. All they could give each other was a conveyance of their feelings through their eyes, the touch of a hand.

Nora Bruce was strangely silent during this time. Lucy had expected her to be more trouble than anyone: it was her perfect opportunity to get her jibes into her son-in-law, but she seemed to have withdrawn into herself, and Lucy could have sworn there was a thoughtful air about her, if such a word could be applied to a woman as eternally restless as she.

Lucy was delighted when Meg was able to come back once more to Moorgate House. She had missed the motherly little woman more than she could have believed possible. She had gone to visit her and Bob in their charming cottage and had been fussed over and made so welcome she was overwhelmed.

She threw her arms round Meg on her first morning back and Meg straightened her hat and patted Lucy's arm. "There, there, my lassie," she said gently, "I've missed you too, and Lorn, the dear laddie. I thought the last time he was over seeing Bob he looked very very unhappy – even more so than usual."

Lucy said nothing and Meg nodded wisely. "It's his lordship, isn't it? Up to his tricks again – pushing Clarrissa to the top of the rainbow only to let her slide down again the minute he's gone. There will be thunderstorms – mark my words – but och, I don't have to tell you that, you've had experience of it already."

Her kindly eyes appraised Lucy fondly. "You're so bonny – and good; no use one without the other. The most perfect-looking flower can hide the worst poison . . ." She shook her head. "Where will it all end – that's what I'd like to know."

She was to get her answer sooner than anyone in the house could have imagined possible. The start of the climax came with a change in the weather. A bitter north-east wind cast an icy breath over the sun's heat and with it came flurries of snow which harried the spring flowers and worried the farmers in the thick of the lambing season.

One morning Lucy got up to look from the window and was met with a white world. She could hardly believe that barely a week before, she and Lorn had sunbathed in the cove and swum in the bay.

The memory of those sun-kissed days came to her with a blinding clarity and her breath caught in her throat. It was so near, yet so much had happened to invade her peace of mind she felt it had all been unreal. But the pain in her heart was real enough, that and the sweet tide of warmth that flooded her being when she looked at the big soft double bed – and remembered.

She went out of her room and met Lorn in the corridor. Their eyes met and held, all their pent-up feelings burning into each other with such strength it was as if they were in a physical embrace.

"I love you, my darling," he whispered. "And I miss you so."

He walked away from her and she reeled with the hurt of wondering how often he would have to walk away from her like that, lonelier than he had ever been, and she unable to go to him and give him comfort.

As she stood there a door clicked quietly nearby and Andrew came out. "It hurts – eh, little Lucy?" he said softly.

"How would you know?" she asked, fighting to keep the tears from welling into her eyes. He was so cruel – and to think she had once imagined she loved him – that he loved her.

"Oh I know alright, honey." His eyes raked her body. "Not in the way you do, or . . ." he inclined his head, "him. I was never soft like big brother, but I hurt in a different way, with my pride, not my heart. That sort of stuff is for fools who enjoy going around nursing their feelings. My pride was hurt by you, Lucy, and I have to make you suffer a wee bit – you must see that, darling."

"Yes, I do see, Andrew. I see how you make us all suffer, especially Clarrissa; you lift her up to the heights then you let her down again with such a jolt she makes Lorn's life a hell for weeks after you've gone."

"Rissa." He said the name jeeringly. "She's just a spoiled brat who's had her own way all her life. . . ."

"Then you make a good team," she threw at him.

"Darling, be a good girl and let me finish. Rissa's a bit like me, always wanting what she can't have. She can't have me – not any more, but it gives her a great kick pining after the grass on the other side. And I can't have you, my sweet darling – not yet anyway – but until I do, just to be near you excites me so much . . ."

"You're despicable, stay away from me!" she cried. She felt frightened by his words, by his arms reaching out to her, and she ran into the bathroom to stand with her back to the door, her heart racing in her breast. Out in the corridor she heard him chuckling, obviously delighted at seeing fear in her.

When she went to Clarrissa's room to get her up she found her in a strangely withdrawn mood and she remembered Clarrissa had been unusually chastened at dinner last night, and all through the evening that followed. "Are you feeling alright, Clarrissa?" she asked.

The older girl raised her head slowly and an odd smile trembled on her lips. "No, darling, I feel like hell, but it's nothing that you can cure. Ask Andrew to come and see me after I've had my bath – tell him to come to my room."

The house was silent when Lucy came downstairs, just after eleven. She heard the outside kitchen door shutting and went in to greet a rosy-cheeked Meg who was shaking the snow from her coat and uttering amazed comments about the change in the weather.

"Sit down," smiled Lucy, "I'll make the tea while you hang up your coat."

They were settled cosily by the table, sipping mugs of steaming tea when Lorn came in rubbing his hands. "It's bitter out there. Who would have thought the weather could change so quickly?"

"Ach, it's all this pollution and nuclear things they have nowadays," said Meg with a shake of her head. "Everything is upside down and no mistake. Sit you down laddie and I'll get you a cuppa—" She broke off suddenly to stare out of the window at the red mail van hurtling recklessly up the slippery drive. "Would you look at the way Hugh Patterson is driving – like a madman! Can something be wrong?"

Lucy and Lorn got to their feet simultaneously, both of them knowing in that instant that Hugh Patterson the postman was the bearer of bad news.

He burst into the kitchen, his normally ruddy face pale with horror, and gasped, "Doctor – come quickly for God's sake! Your wife – her car has gone over the road two miles back. I got here as fast as I could – nearly killed myself in the process. . . ." Unable to say anything more he collapsed into a chair to regain his breath. Lorn was already snatching up his bag; Meg rushing to fill flasks with hot drinks; Lucy fleeing up the hall to fetch blankets from the linen cupboard, her mind racing frantically.

At this hour of the day Clarrissa was normally in her room, resting before lunch, but she must have gone out, made her way to the garage and taken the car without telling anyone . . . and in this weather!

But why? why? why? The question clamoured around

in her head. She recalled how Clarrissa had been earlier, and her words: *I feel like hell, but it's nothing you can cure . . . tell Andrew to come . . .*

Lucy had told Andrew that he was wanted in Clarrissa's room and she remembered how sickened she had been at the expression of disgust on his face and at his words: "Not the brat again! God, can't that woman leave me alone? I made it quite plain yesterday . . ."

He had stomped off without finishing the sentence, leaving Lucy bewildered and angry.

Something had happened between the two but she had no earthly idea what it was. She burst into the sitting room where Andrew and Nora Bruce were ensconced, both sitting apart from each other and both of them silent. "Quickly!" Lucy hardly recognised her own voice. "Clarrissa's had an accident in her car!"

They stood up at the same time, Nora Bruce's hands fluttering to her mouth, her eyes wide with shock; Andrew staring at Lucy, an indefinable expression on his face. He said nothing but Nora Bruce began to babble, "Oh my darling little girl! She wasn't herself! I knew it, I knew . . ."

Meg came bustling through to phone for an ambulance and she told the hysterical woman in no uncertain terms. "Ach, stop your havering and get along to see if you can be of some use. Your lassie needs you and the doctor is waiting to go."

Lucy, carrying the blankets, met him in the hall. His face was white, the muscle in his jaw was working. "Good girl," he said, when he saw the blankets. Briefly his hand gripped hers. "Hugh has gone to fetch the police and will guide them back to the place."

His hand tightened on hers, then they were running

outside to his car. The engine was still warm and started readily. He hardly waited for Andrew to slam the rear doors before he was off, slipping and skidding down the drive to the road.

It was an interminable journey, for although the roads were clear of snow, slush and icy ruts made them treacherous. Lorn crouched over the wheel, silent as were they all but for Nora Bruce, who was sobbing into her hanky and muttering over and over, "My darling, my poor darling, my baby . . ."

"Oh, for God's sake, woman," snapped Andrew at one point. "You're not going to help anyone, much less your daughter, if you keep that up. Get a grip on yourself."

She sniffed loudly and said coldly, "That's something you're very good at, isn't it, Andrew? Always in control, never letting the mask slip . . ."

"Please, don't let's have a character analysis now," gritted Lorn, "save your strength for what's ahead."

After that a grim silence descended over everyone and no one spoke another word till they arrived at the accident spot and the car slewed to a crazy halt.

Clarrissa's car had veered off the road and had come to rest violently on the rocky shore. It was tilted to one side, the driver's door swinging backwards and forwards in the wind. Clarrissa had somehow managed to open it and get out. She lay among the rocks. She hadn't even taken time to stop and don a jacket. Hugh had covered her with his, but it was a pitifully inadequate insulation against the icy wind blowing in from the sea.

Lucy followed on Lorn's heels and felt a great sadness in her. Clarrissa, beautiful Clarrissa, looked like an abandoned rag doll. Her face was a mass of cuts and bruises, but her dark eyes were open, staring at Lorn as he gave her a swift examination.

Lucy was wrapping blankets round her, holding a cup filled with hot tea to her mouth, directing her to sip it slowly, all the while speaking in a soft but reassuring voice. Gently she took Clarrissa's hands. They were like ice.

Lorn was kneeling on the wet sand, Clarrissa's head cradled on his knee. "Hush, hush," he told her soothingly, "you mustn't try to talk. I'm here, we're all here."

"Thank God." The words were a mere sigh on Clarrissa's white lips, and then she closed her eyes, her entire body growing limp and heavy in her husband's comforting embrace.

Chapter Twenty-one

Nora Bruce took one look at her daughter's deathly pale face and turned away. Whimpering like a wounded puppy she stumbled off to lean on some rocks and weep copiously into her hanky. Of Andrew there was no sign.

"Lorn," Clarrissa spoke again. His name on her lips was soft but strong. "Oh what the hell!" Her voice was suddenly full of vigour. "Don't try and shut me up. You're not going to stop me doing the grand finale bit!" Her frozen lips cracked into a smile. "Lorn – I've been a stupid bitch. I wanted Andrew to take me back with him – to London. I asked him yesterday – and – again this morning – but – do you know what he said . . .?" She shivered, and Lucy held her hands tightly under the blankets. "He said, 'Like hell I will. Who wants to be lumbered with a write-off?'."

The tears were spilling down over her waxen cheeks and she gave a short bitter laugh. "We're both alike Andrew and I – both takers – both losers. You've been very sweet to me, dear Lorn. Forgive me, bitch that I am, for making your life a misery. I was leaving you for him – I love him you see – he's a swine, but I love him to bits."

Her long fingers curled round Lucy's. "You and Lorn are made for each other – I know you love him – don't waste time mooning around – grab him while the going's good."

She struggled to raise her head. "Andrew, where is he? I want – to curse the hell out of him."

Nora Bruce's sobs were growing more intense and Clarrissa murmured sardonically, "Typical Mother – she always did cry at the wrong time – save the tears for later, Mother dear."

The snowflakes were whirling, dropping and melting on her dark hair. Lorn brushed them away and said firmly, "You're going to be alright, Clarrissa. I've examined you thoroughly, and apart from a few cuts and bruises I can find nothing wrong— "

Impatiently she pushed his hand away and cried petulantly, "Lorn, how can you say that? I'm dying! I know I'm dying – and there's something I have to tell you first!"

"You are *not* dying, Clarrissa; you are just cold and shaken. The ambulance will be here shortly and you'll be fine in no time."

Lucy stood up and saw Andrew, standing above on the grass verge, a dark looming figure without emotion or pity. With blinding clarity she realised that he was the spider in the web. All along she had imagined it to be Nora Bruce, but the weak, pitiful woman crying helplessly nearby was just another victim of his venomous charm.

Andrew had touched all their lives with that, had charmed – and taken. Clarrissa had become so mesmerised by him she had allowed herself to be fully taken in by him – yet – he was the only one who could really handle her. He was a match for her in every way. . . .

He was coming down the slope, straight over to Clarrissa, his eyes hard and unsympathetic as he gazed down at her. "C'mon, Rissa, enough of the dying swan act," he told her harshly. "Open your eyes and look at me."

"I don't want to talk to you," she said sulkily.

"Maybe not but you're damned well going to listen! You've done it again, haven't you? The prima donna act. I've a hunch I wouldn't be far wrong if I said you arranged all this to bring attention on yourself. Oh yes, you can look as innocent and as indignant as you like, but it's true! You knew when you drove the car out of the garage just exactly what you were going to do! You're a damned good driver, Rissa. It was very easy to stage this little set-up. Nothing too drastic – just enough of a little drama to get yourself noticed. . . ." He gave an amused snort of laughter.

Clarrissa's eyes were wide with rage. "Lorn, tell him to stop, tell him to stop it, Lorn."

But Andrew came closer, his eyes glittering like blue ice. "No, Rissa, I'm damned if I'll stop! I meant what I said last night, and again this morning. I don't want anything to do with you till you stop all this play-acting and get up off your backside and *walk*, Rissa!"

He bent down and with a violent jerk threw back the blankets to expose her legs. "Move your legs, Rissa!" he ordered harshly. "You can do it! How else are we to believe you got out of the car? You crawled out, didn't you? Crawled, moved, scrambled, take your pick, but you did one of them in order to arrange yourself prettily amongst the seaweed. It's true, isn't it? Isn't it, Rissa? You had a good idea when Hugh would be coming along so that you wouldn't have to wait too long to be rescued. We all know how much you hate to be uncomfortable, and hanging around on a sodden beach isn't exactly anybody's idea of fun."

Clarrissa was moving her head from side to side. "No! No! No!" she screamed.

"Oh yes, yes, yes, Rissa! Now – move your legs. If you do – just one tiny bit – then I promise to take you away with me – get you into a hospital in London where you can learn to walk again."

Nora Bruce came forward, her face white with outrage, but Lorn, who had moved with Lucy further up the shore, put out a hand to stop her. "Leave them," he ordered quictly. "This is maybe just the thing Clarrissa needs."

"But – my poor darling . . ." began Nora Bruce. Lorn's grip on her arm tightened and she winced.

"Your poor darling won't thank you if you say anything now," said Lorn tensely. "Look at her – she's moving her legs."

It was true. Clarrissa was white-faced, trembling; tears were rolling down her checks; every muscle in her body was quivering as, with a supreme effort, she moved one foot a fraction.

Sobbing and panting she moved it again, then she fell back, totally drained, but as she gazed at Andrew a smile of triumph lifted the corners of her lovely mouth.

His handsome face broke into a grin and he fell down on his knees beside her to take her in his arms. "I knew you could do it – I knew you *would* do it – for me. We're made for one another, Rissa. In days to come we'll yell at one another; tear each other's eyes out; maybe even part now and then – but always you'll come back to me."

She put her hands over her face. "You're a swine, Andrew Graham," she told him shakily. "A callous, hard-hearted swine."

He merely laughed. "You're an able match for me, Rissa – and just think: we'll dance again you and I –

because you're going to get better quite quickly; I'm going to see to that."

A large patch of blue had appeared in the sky, the sun was pushing its golden rays over the earth; a curlew's song echoed over the sea. Lucy felt that the sudden change in the weather signified a good omen. She turned her head to see Lorn's eyes on her and she saw love, pure and real, a love that would always be there – for her.

The ambulance arrived, followed closely by a police car. The men came down the beach and soon Clarrissa was being carried on a stretcher up to the ambulance. She was complaining loudly, telling the men to do this, that, and the next thing, but when she passed Lucy a smile touched her mouth and she closed one eyelid in a slow, deliberate wink.

Clarrissa was kept in hospital for two days. On the morning she was due to come home, Lorn and Lucy were in the sitting room with Nora Bruce, Andrew having left to collect Clarrissa.

"Lorn, I have something to tell you." Nora Bruce's voice was unusually soft. "Clarrissa tried to tell you on the beach at the time of her accident, but never quite got it out. It has to do with her and Andrew."

Lucy stood up. "I think I had better go – if it's personal . . ."

"No, dear, sit down." The words and tone of voice were kind, almost humble. "Clarrissa thinks very highly of you, you know. She – when she sent you back here from the nursing home she told me she was doing it as – as a joke. Well, you know Clarrissa. But she also said to me that she knew you and Lorn were a perfect match and she hoped things would work out for you. She was planning at the time to go away with Andrew – only – I – I didn't take it seriously." She sniffed and straightened her shoulders. "It wasn't the first time she had said it – and I – oh foolish woman that I am – encouraged her – but that was before she told me . . ."

She paused, and looked at Lorn for a long moment. "She told me that the child wasn't yours, Lorn; it was Andrew's. Do you remember that time she came to stay with me in London for some weeks? It happened then. Oh, I knew she was seeing him. She used to come home sparkling – well, you know how she loves theatres, parties, dances. He escorted her to them all.

"I didn't imagine there was anything else – a flirtation perhaps; nothing more serious. When she discovered she was pregnant she said nothing to Andrew and came back here – to you. She pretended the baby was yours, that it was born prematurely, and it was such a tiny mite it may well have been. But it wasn't – it was a full-term baby. Andrew's child . . . I'm sorry, Lorn."

"Did he know the child was his?" Lorn's voice was very low.

"Yes, according to Clarissa he knew, but he never came near her till last Christmas and – she accepted his desertion of her at a time when she most needed him because she knew that to do otherwise could have meant losing him altogether, and she could never have borne that.

"She poured out her heart to me when she was at the nursing home. She had bottled it all up for so long, and I think the time had come for her to cleanse her mind."

Lorn had put a trembling hand over his eyes and Lucy's heart went out to him in his agony. "But why – why?" he cried, in an anguish of soul. "Why did she blame me

211

– hate me – make me feel I was guilty of something I didn't do?"

Nora Bruce looked down at her hands. "It was the only way she could make her own guilt bearable. The torture in her found release by torturing you; the more she twisted the knife in you the less it hurt her. You were her pin-cushion, Lorn, and—" Her voice broke. "Unwittingly I abetted her. I liked Andrew you see, was taken in by him . . ."

She stood up, a much chastened woman. "Strangely enough – despite everything – I still like him; he's a very likeable person. It will take me some time though to forgive him for all the hurt he's caused us all. My bags are packed. I'm going off with Andrew and Clarrissa. I must look after her till she is quite well. After that – who knows . . . I need to find a place for myself; build up my own life again. After all . . ." her lips twisted into a rueful smile, "Clarrissa is a big girl now, and I must let her go her own way."

Tyres crunched on the gravel driveway; a car door banged. Nora Bruce jumped and said hastily, "I'd better go and help Clarrissa – she'll need some tea before the journey. Lucy, would you come with me and give a hand?"

Lucy knew the reason behind the request; knew what was going to happen in the next few minutes. Lorn was on his feet, his eyes black in his tense face. The cork was about to erupt from the bottle, and she knew that there was nothing that she, anyone, could do to stop it!

Andrew passed them in the hall and went straight upstairs without a word. Lucy put her hand on Lorn's arm but he shook her off and bounded upstairs to explode into his brother's room.

212

Andrew turned from his cases, his blue eyes mocking. "Why, if it isn't big brother. Ever think of knocking—" Lorn's knuckles crashed into his jaw and he was sent flying across the room to lie sprawled over the bed, fury flooding his eyes when he drew his hand across his mouth and saw blood.

"Why you—" He had no time to say more. Lorn was pulling him up, his fists cracking against flesh and bone again and again till the younger man was sagging at the knees and sobbing like a little boy. "No more, please, Lorn, no more," he begged.

Lorn's chest was heaving, his breath was ragged in his throat. "No need to tell you what that was for," he panted. "It was something that was long overdue. Now get out – and stay out! I don't want you to cast your shadow over my door again."

Andrew was recovering. "I don't intend to, old son, I only go where there's wine, women, and song." He looked about him contemptuously, "And there's precious little of that in this hole in the corner."

He picked up his cases and began to walk away, but at the door he turned, a little smile hovering at the corners of his bleeding mouth, as he said softly, "You're right, Lorn, I did have it coming. In some strange way I feel better – everything out in the open at last. . . ."

The smile broadened. "I'm doing you a favour, you know, taking Rissa off your hands. The little bitch takes some handling – yet – I love her. I've loved her all along, I suppose, and now I've got the vixen. . . ."

He gave a short laugh. "It will be quite a challenge, taming a woman like that but I think I might really enjoy it. When everything's settled I'll marry her – can't tame a wildcat without cornering it first."

He ran lightly downstairs. Clarrissa turned at his approach, her eyes widening at the sight of his swollen mouth, then her gaze travelled beyond him to Lorn.

"So – you know." Her voice was flat, without emotion, then she propelled her chair forward and sat for a long moment gazing up at the tall, strong figure of her husband. He gazed back at her, his dark eyes steady and unwavering.

"You're quite a man, Lorn Campbell," she said at last, her voice low and husky. "I'm sorry, really sorry for all the bitchy things I've ever said and done to you. You deserve better than me – and . . ." she slid Lucy a sidelong glance, "I think somehow you're going to get it. Goodbye, Lorn dearest – and – be happy."

He smiled then, his brown eyes full of warmth. "You too, Clarrissa, the results of your tests came in the morning post. It's good news: there's no physical reason why you shouldn't be up on your feet in a month or two – dancing the hours away. As you were meant to," he finished softly.

Andrew was stamping with impatience. "Come on, Rissa," he said brusquely. "We've a long journey ahead of us and I'm damned if I'll wait a minute longer for you."

"But – I haven't had my tea yet *and* I really ought to rest for a while. Don't you have any consideration at all, Andrew Graham?" Her voice was high, petulant. Without a word Andrew grabbed the handles of her chair and began to propel her outside. As she passed she reached out to grab at Lucy's hand, a gleam of delight dancing in her eyes. "Lucy, isn't he a perfect beast? Come with me, do, and wave me goodbye."

When she was settled in the car she held on to Lucy's hand for a long moment. "I've enjoyed having you for a

214

nanny. Oh, there, I'm doing it again: being bitchy – but – I don't really mean it. I *have* enjoyed knowing you, Lucy Pemberton."

Her glance took in Lorn standing a little distance away. "You'll give him everything I never could. I don't have to tell you to be happy, I know you will be."

Lucy turned away and bumped into Andrew, who caught her arm and smiled down at her. "It was nice knowing you, little Lucy Pemberton. Try not to think too badly of me. I'm sorry if I hurt you." His grin flashed. "I was never a good sport – I hated the idea of you getting off the hook – the only one of my girls who ever got away – that wanted to."

Nora Bruce got into the car, doors slammed; a few minutes later the peach-coloured Mercedes roared away down the drive and out of the gates of Moorgate House. Lucy watched it go and felt weak with relief. She felt as if a veil had been lifted and she was seeing daylight for the first time in months. She wandered into the house. It was silent again, the way it was when it had been just herself and Lorn sharing it.

He found her at the back of the house, standing on the lawn, gazing out to a bright horizon that flecked the sea with gold. Without a word he slipped his arm round her slender waist. She could feel the relaxation in him but didn't turn to look at him. Instead she kept her eyes on the dazzling stretch of sea. She spoke his name, her voice very low. "Lorn."

"Yes, darling?"

"You know I can't stay here any longer – not in the same house as you. I'll – I'll have to go away."

Gently he turned her face towards his and kissed away

the tears glistening on her eyelashes. "My sweet little Lucy. Dear, dear little Lucy," he murmured huskily. "Meg and I have arranged it all between us. You're to go and stay with her; she has a lovely spare bedroom. The walls are all done with rose-sprinkled paper and there's a bed piled to the ceiling with feather mattresses. She needs a bit of help with Bob. He'll fairly love having a beautiful young nurse to tend him hand and foot. Also . . ." his arm tightened round her waist, "Elspeth is leaving next month to be married. I'm going to need someone to help me out in the surgery. Do you think . . . would you consider taking us all in hand?"

His hand was warm on her arm, and in the brown depths of his eyes she saw pure love, embracing her, touching her soul with its tender beauty. They kissed, and it was a kiss that diffused her entire being, flooding her with a joy that could never be surpassed.

She didn't need words to let him know what her answer was. In a dream she felt herself walking with him, safe in the circle of his arms as he guided her over the lawns to the little cove where the wavelets lapped their toes and chuckled over the white pebbles. They stood for a moment, his dark head against her golden curls, each of them aware of the wildness and beauty of the ocean beating against the timeless shores of Kintyre. Then he gathered her into his arms, to kiss her, and hold her as if he could never bear to let her go. She snuggled against him and murmured softly, "This is where I belong, Lorn: here, with you. I'll never leave you; you'll never get rid of me now. I'm here for keeps."

His deep laugh was music in her ears. "My dear little Lucy Pemberton," he murmured. "Somehow I don't think you're going to get rid of me either, so we're stuck with one another – for keeps – and somehow I don't think I'm going to mind one bit."

She took a deep breath and laid her head on his shoulder. "Always to be here – with you." She sighed contentedly and the song in her heart was ecstasy.

THE POPPY FIELD